Eileen Tierney Baker is a writer and educator. She is an avid reader and is fascinated with true crime and history. She currently resides in Alexandria, Kentucky, with her husband, Gary, and their children, Zack and Madelyn Kate. This is her first publication.

For Mom
Your Bean loves you always.

Eileen Tierney Baker

THE DEVIL WALKS IN DAYLIGHT

AUSTIN MACAULEY PUBLISHERS™

LONDON • CAMBRIDGE • NEW YORK • SHARJAH

Ordering Information:
Quantity sales: special discounts are available on quantity purchases by corporations, associations, and others. For details, contact the publisher at the address below.

Publisher's Cataloging-in-Publication data
Baker, Eileen Tierney
The Devil Walks in Daylight

ISBN 9781645362173 (Paperback)
ISBN 9781645362180 (Hardback)
ISBN 9781645368519 (ePub e-book)

Library of Congress Control Number: 2019920977

www.austinmacauley.com/us

First Published (2020)
Austin Macauley Publishers LLC
40 Wall Street, 28th Floor
New York, NY 10005
USA

mail-usa@austinmacauley.com
+1 (646) 5125767

I want to thank my mother, Barbara Kehew, who was always there to talk about Dietrich and Vika, and listen as their stories unfolded. You are still with me, Mom, every day.

I also want to thank my son, Zachary, who is not only wise, but also a bold truth-teller. My daughters, Hannah, who pushed me to move forward, even when I didn't want to, and Madelyn Kate, who is the best encourager. And, of course, my husband, Gary, who is my partner in absolutely everything.

Historical Disclaimer

The following story takes place in Europe, spanning from W.W.I. to W.W.I.I. It speculates on the unsolved murders of the Gruber family at Hinterkaifeck in 1922. Some names have been modified or changed. All demonstrations and conclusions are purely speculations. This is a work of fiction.

Prologue

If love were a color, it would be blue. Blue like the water in the creek that ran through the east end of town. Blue like the spring sky. Blue like her eyes: enveloping, satiating, and endless.

This was not love – although the look in his eyes as he turned to see my first blow did set my heart a flutter ever so slightly. His face exploded in time with my rage. Again. His nose disappeared with the lower half of his jaw. He fell, twitching, as if his body was not quite sure how to respond to such brutal force. Eventually, it stopped. I did not.

I was covered; covered in his filth and metallic stench. It painted the walls and bathed the floor. I would wash it off. He never could, not living, not dead. His depravity was embedded in his very soul (which about this time should be meeting a very angry maker). I wiped my face with the back of my hand and shook off the blood as I stepped outside.

If justice were a color, it would be red.

Chapter 1
1915, Hinterkaifeck, the Return

She stood motionless in the afternoon sun, the wind freeing strands of her dark hair from the bobby pins that secured it neatly on top of her head, leaving wisps of the rescued hair lightly flogging her face with all the strength of an angry toddler. She did not appear to notice or to care.

Vika clutched the bundle tightly in her arms, unsure of her next move. She had promised herself she would never return here, yet here she was. She had sworn it to God himself, on her knees, in front of her silver crucifix that hung above her marital bed. The crucifix had been a family heirloom given to her on her wedding day: the corpus tarnished and gray, with the arms outstretched unnaturally. It always made her smile, as if Jesus were coming in for a big hug. She had prayed before it, thanking God for freeing her from this place, for the chance at something better. She had been quite wrong about the something better, and now life had brought her back to this doorway, less than two years after vowing never to cross this threshold again. Both the reason to stay and the reason to run away rested quietly in her arms, wiggling and cooing delicately. "Ssshhh," Vika whispered softly, almost immediately soothing the child back into a peaceful slumber.

Looking around, she took in the scenery. It was deceptively beautiful. Lush, full trees bordered the farmland, separating it from the surrounding forest. The deeply shaded grass and the bare birch tree, by the path that led up to the main house, begged to be immortalized in a painting; to be hung above a fireplace and gazed upon with fondness and envy of a simpler time. The atmosphere was one of peace and incorruptibility – to the uneducated eye. Her eyes had seen the underbelly of the land she stood on, and it was far from incorrupt.

The farmhouse itself was impressive as well, three stories (including the large attic), followed by the barn and the stables. Its size and function were quite grand. Here, the human element corroded everything it touched.

Even in these depressing economic times, Vika was not concerned over her parent's financial ability to take her home, even with added stress of a baby to feed. Neither was there an issue of space, as the farmhouse was spacious and only sheltered her parents and their maid, Zenzi.

No, Vika's concerns, the ones that kept her from rapping on the front door for the better part of an hour now, lied elsewhere; somewhere dark and unholy, where the only ones to hear her screams were the very ones who caused them to be uttered in the first place. A place where she feared God would not even come to find her again.

She was torn. She had nowhere else to go, and the bundle to care for now. Taking a deep breath, she stepped closer to the door, reciting her justifications in her head, as she had continuously since her decision to come home: *I am an adult now, I can protect us, it is only for a while – just temporary*, and finally the hard truth – *I have no other choice.*

She knocked quickly on the solid oak door, afraid to change her mind yet again. After all this time, just entering would seem presumptuous.

The door opened and the imposing form of her father filled the frame. Instinctually, she took a step back. One might think, a father, on such an occasion as his little girl returning home, would smile and welcome her and his new grandchild into his arms and his home. One would be wrong.

He looked down at her, even being close in height, Andrew Gruber, had always had the ability to make himself appear taller, larger. He loomed over people, creating a physical dominance, morphing them into errant schoolchildren. As if on cue, Vika felt twelve years old, rather than her twenty-eight years; she was instantly unsure, fearful, and unworthy – exactly the effect her father intended. Score one for Andrew.

His mouth was set in a permanent frown. It was fitting, as he always seemed to find dissatisfaction in absolutely everything in life. Moving north from his mouth sat an uneven brown mustache that Vika used to trim back in the day, but he clearly had taken over that task for himself now. A sharply pointed nose and two close-set black eyes settled on his furrowed eyebrows that looked her over critically.

"Hello, Father," she croaked. *Bad start*, she thought. It was all part of his intimidation strategy to make her speak first. She knew this but choked on her fear of him anyway. Score two for Andrew, Vika – zero. Oh, when will logic trump emotions in the confrontation of wills? In this particular case, never, but she always hoped. Void of emotions, her father would always win.

"So you've come home." He stood there, stating the obvious, putting his hands in his coat pockets and rocking slightly back on his heels, yet still not inviting her inside.

"I'll only be here for a little while, Father, until I get back on my feet again." Vika was already apologizing for her imposition, even though, legally, the farm was hers.

"This?" he nodded toward the bundle sleeping peacefully in her arms.

"This is Celie, your granddaughter. Isn't she perfect?" She held her up for him to admire, as she slept contentedly, her round chubby cheeks moving in rhythm as she sucked her thumb. She was an angel.

Vika's father was not impressed. He glanced briefly, not admiring, not doting. (Again, she did not so much expect that as foolishly hoped.) Andrew simply turned to his side, signaling his permission for her to enter. He did not move any farther, causing Vika to have to brush solidly against him as she passed. With her back to him and Celie clutched to her chest, she scooted inside with her bag. She did not miss Andrew's sharp intake of breath against the back of her neck or the bristly brush of his mustache. She closed her eyes and choked down the sickness rising in her throat. *I am an adult now, I can protect us, it is only for a while – just temporary, and I have no other choice.* She repeated what had become something of a mantra for her repeatedly in her head as Andrew firmly shut the door behind them.

Chapter 2
Munich, 1918, the Departure

Wow, Dietrich, you have really messed things up this time. He thought to himself as his train left the station. He never imagined he would leave Munich, let alone leave under the circumstances that he did. It was too late now, too late to go back. He wondered how many decisions in life are actually preplanned. Do we really make our own decisions, or is that an illusion to disguise the fact that life's circumstances lead us around, with its fingers up our nostrils like a schoolyard bully?

Dietrich intended to stay in Munich forever: be a successful banker, find a beautiful woman, and raise a hoard of kids. There was nothing exotic or unusual about his plan. It was the same as many young men his age, but he wasn't there. Instead, he was riding in a musty, cramped train, with his only possessions fitting into a small rucksack, picking at the chipping black paint around his window, and watching the tree-lined tracks rush by.

"Charles Blakely, get over here now!" A young-ish mother, a few seats up from Dietrich, was frantically trying to wrangle in her son, a freckled-faced scamp (he had never used that word before, but it seemed to fit the boy perfectly) with a curly mop of bright red hair. She had him by the strap of his lederhosen, which had come unbuttoned in his mad rush to escape. She kept roping her hands around the loose strap as if reeling in a thrashing fish. The boy reminded him of that boy in that O'Henry's story, *The Ransom of Red Chief* (a pretty good writer for a Yank). Dietrich bet his mother wished for some eager kidnappers right about now.

Her age was difficult to determine. At first glance, she seemed very young; however, lines etched her face with worry and disappointment, causing wrinkles to appear ahead of schedule. Still, there was no gray in her hair. It is appalling what life's circumstances can do to the faces of the pretty. He guessed her to be in her late twenties, but she looked at least ten years older.

Red Chief finally wriggled away and darted down the aisle of the train past Dietrich. His mother let him go, her weary face alerting anyone who glanced over at her that he was their problem now. She sat back in her seat, letting out a heavy breath. Dietrich wondered where she was going, if possibly, she too, was running away from something.

He lapsed back into depressed reflection. There was so much he wanted to change; it just wasn't possible. *Move on, move forward; leave it behind.* He repeated the words in his head, hoping that he would begin to believe them. He would begin fresh, start a life of which he could be proud. If only he could forget what he just left in Munich, maybe, just maybe, it would be possible.

A red-faced steward came charging up the aisle with an amused Red Chief by the back collar (Dietrich wondered for a moment how much of this child's life was spent having people cart him around by his clothing?). The steward stood for a moment in front of the mother's seat to assure himself of her attention (and his displeasure) before dropping her son in the seat next to her with a shameful stare. She nodded apologetically in reply and appeared to try to bribe the boy with some hard candy. It must have worked because this time, he stayed in his seat.

The sun was just beginning to set behind the far-off mountain range. Dietrich's eyes closed and he relented, he wasn't driving the damn train. He was alone. He was really alone: no more family, no friends, just him and his questionable future. He had no idea where he was headed. He was going away, that was as far as he had gotten in his plan. He would ride this train to its last stop and take it from there.

What was he going to do? How would he survive? He tried to block these rational questions from his thoughts and just focus on the scenery outside his window. The thoughts kept invading his mind, though. All he had ever known was working in his family's bakery. He had left what little money he had behind with his brother, and hadn't any contacts in the surrounding cities.

Dietrich was unsure of everything. There was only one thing that was unfailingly clear – he was not going back. He couldn't go back. He would follow this lonely road as far as it would take him. Anywhere had to be better than what he left behind.

What a fool he was to believe that.

Chapter 3
Vika and Karl

Karl would be home any minute and Vika wanted everything to be perfect. She had just finished putting on her rarely applied makeup and pulled the curlers from her long dark hair, allowing it to cascade in smooth trundles over her shoulders. Her jade green dress clung attractively to her curves and complimented her fair skin.

The roast was in the oven. He loved roast. They could rarely afford it, but it was his favorite. What an outstanding surprise to let him know she was thinking of him. He loved the little red potatoes and she imagined how he would smile when he saw all the effort she had gone to today. As the potatoes boiled, she chopped cabbage. She was going to be the best wife ever. He would have no room to find fault. The better part of the day had been spent waxing the floors and dusting. The house smelled like fresh lilac and Honeysuckle she had picked from outside earlier that day. This was going to work.

Hours passed as she waited, eventually falling into a restless sleep at the table. The sound of the slamming door abruptly woke her. The remaining stubs of the candles she had lit earlier still cast a dim glow that illuminated the stumbling figure of her husband, Karl, falling through the front door. She could smell from where she sat the potent stench of cheap beer and even cheaper perfume.

"Where have you been?" Vika demanded as she stood. She couldn't help herself. She was angry and frustrated at all of her great efforts going to waste.

"Pub," he hiccupped. "Why the hell do you care?" He made his way to the table and picked up what remained of the now cold and dry roast with one meaty paw, taking a large, crude bite. "Cold," he mumbled, "Tastes like shit."

"It wasn't cold at suppertime, when I made it for you, when I expected you to be home," Vika shot back.

"Ate at the pub," his incoherence was becoming more evident, "You keeping tabs on me?"

Vika sank back in her chair. This was going nowhere. There was no use in arguing, besides, he wouldn't remember any of this tomorrow. He shuffled awkwardly to their bedroom and she listened to him bump into things, until he finally collapsed on their bed. Let him.

This was her final attempt, and she had been so hopeful. She did not want him to go off to fight in the war with their marriage falling apart. She still had two weeks before he left and she wanted to create some semblance of happiness in their relationship before he left. She was hoping her special announcement at dinner that night would be their new beginning.

He could have the bed tonight, she was not about to go into that room and share it with him and his dirty, rank stench. *And I will keep the news to myself,* she thought, as she pressed her hands lovingly to her stomach. Tonight had been such a disaster, she just didn't know what she would do if he wasn't happy about the baby. With her mind made up, Vika laid her head back down on the kitchen table, settling in for the night.

*****

No matter what Vika tried to create or delude herself into believing about her marriage, it had been a farce from the beginning, and more of a family merger than a bonding of love. She had reluctantly entered into the union thinking the only obstacles were her feelings. Her mother had told her that she could love Karl if she worked at it. Vika decided she would work very hard.

However, her lack of emotion for her husband was just the beginning of their many problems. Abuse and cheating followed; Karl drank all the time. She discovered that she was not the only one in this 'merger' that wasn't in love. There was no love between Karl and her. She had hoped and truly believed she could force it. The truth was, as inept as she was, she really wanted love, a true romantic partnership, children, cooking dinner for her husband, playing with her children, keeping house. It was not very 'forward thinking,' but it was what her heart had always wanted. Since she was pushed into marriage with Karl, she hoped to make the best of it.

Their wedding night was not expected. She envisioned tenderness, fumbling laughter, and a connection of souls. That it was not. It was quick, *Thank God for that.* He was rough, demanding, and completely oblivious to her innocence and fear. He took her, ripped her, left her bruised and bleeding on the bed, and went to the tavern down the road to drink the rest of the evening. 'Till death do us part.'

The marriage did not improve from there. The one and only bright spot, the only part that Vika could never regret, was the conception of her beautiful

16

little girl, Celie. She was her eternal blessing, her hope for a future, and her reason to get up and face life every day; with God's help, her daughter would never, NEVER, go through what she had. Vika would take her failings and pain and use them to ensure a beautiful life for her baby girl.

Karl never developed compassion for his wife. She made the mistake of confronting him once on his 'dalliances.' He had swung and backhanded her so suddenly, that she could not even brace herself for the impact. He blamed her ineptitude as a wife and lover for forcing him to go elsewhere. The encounter ended with her bleeding and apologizing, while his cheating continued, never to be questioned again.

After all of the traumatic experiences within her marriage, finally, Vika experienced widowhood, which, God forgive her, was a relief. With God's infinite mercy, death came sooner than later. Karl died a war hero, with nobody questioning his heroism and honor; and Vika, newly pregnant and now alone, was released from the hell to which she had been assigned.

Her only option right now, was not her top choice, but it was her only choice; she had to move back home. Her parents could afford to take her on and her soon-to-be little girl, and they could use her as a farm hand on their acreage. It would give Celie a family to grow up around. Vika no longer dreamed of a romantic relationship and a brood of children scampering around her feet as she cooked dinner. No, Vika's dream of a having a happy marriage someday was buried deeply beneath screams, betrayal, and the damage of her first union.

Vika stopped reminiscing on what got her here and looked around her childhood bedroom, at the farmhouse, as she sat on the bed with her daughter. How had so much happened, and happened so badly in such a short span of time? Here she was, back home with a child of her own, and no clue about her future. She had envisioned herself at this age so differently. She fully intended to never darken her father's doorstep again, yet here she sat.

She swaddled Celie who lay on the bed in front of her. She carried her tenderly to the bassinette that sat at the end of her bed. Her mother had provided it as a small welcome for her. It was appreciated.

Closing the door, she walked into the hallway and immediately (and literally) ran into Zenzi.

"Watch out!" the family maid scolded.

"Sorry, my fault," Vika wanted to start out on the right foot. "It is good to see you. You are looking well."

"I am well. We all have been well since you left." Zenzi's distaste for Vika was clear and unmasked.

"Look, Zenzi, I am not here to cause problems for anyone or make more work for you…"

"But you will nonetheless." There had always been a sense of rivalry that came from Zenzi over the years, almost of a sibling sort. They were close in years and Zenzi always seemed a bit threatened by the fact that she was an employee, while Vika was the child and heir.

Okay, then. Vika tried a firmer approach, "However, this farm is legally mine, and you are the family maid. You work for the Gruber family, and that includes me. Now, let's try to get along."

Zenzi's attitude shifted. She knew she had pushed too far. "Yes, Ma'am," she replied properly contrite. With her eyes downcast to the floor, she hurried down the hallway.

Vika continued into the kitchen to see her mother. "Hi, Mother." She gripped her shoulders lightly and kissed her cheek. She felt her mother flinch initially and stiffen at the loving gesture. Theirs was not an emotionally satisfying relationship, as much as Vika pushed for it to be so through the years. Her mother was not, well, maternal. She did not kiss boo-boos or hug heartbroken teens as they grieved over their first unrequited schoolyard crush. It wasn't that she didn't want to (this is what Vika told herself.), Cas Gruber just didn't know how.

Thinking this way left room for Vika to dream that someday, she would open that emotional vault and have a genuine, loving relationship with her mother. This delusional thinking kept Vika full of eternal hope and frequent disappointment. For whatever the reasons were, Cas Gruber was not going to return that affection, not ever.

Unbelievably, there was a time when her father started to strike her, that she thought, in some twisted way, that her mother and she could bond over their shared abuse. That wasn't so either. Cas neither intervened nor acknowledged her daughter's mistreatment. She would remove herself to her bedroom, mumbling about her 'headaches.'

"Thank you for the beautiful bassinette. Celie is sleeping soundly," Vika tried again.

"It's fine. Just make sure you find out what your father intends for you to do on the farm in the morning. You'll be working the farm as well as taking care of that baby."

"I know. I'm sure you'll want to spend some time with your granddaughter, also. She's a perfect little angel."

Cas wiped her hands on a kitchen towel. "When I have time," she dismissed the request, "So much work to do around here, you know." Cas left

18

the kitchen, leaving Vika with one more failed attempt to bond, to tuck away in her sadness closet.

Why are you like this? Vika thought, as she heard her mother's bedroom door close.

Chapter 4
Andrew and Cas, 1887

Snakes rarely showed themselves before they were ready to strike. They tended to slither silently, sizing up their prey, weaving themselves in with the grass and trees, making themselves appear, if only for a moment, just as docile and harmless as their surroundings. That was until it was time to prove their dominance over their prey. Until it was time to eat.

Cas Gruber learned this lesson the hard way.

Andrew had once courted her properly. He was nice, romantic, polite, and respectful of her parents. He laughed off the issues of her heightened age and previous marriage and children, as she laughed off the rumors of his gruff and boorish exterior. She knew her position did not make her a 'great catch,' yet it seemed to propel Andrew toward the idea of marriage sooner than later.

In hindsight, Cas questioned Andrew's swiftness to make her his wife, but she hated the idea of widowhood and raising children on her own. It had been mere months since her husband's passing, yet whatever Andrew's reasons, she was ready.

The engagement was quick, the marriage and ensuing pregnancies even quicker. In fact, Vika came on the scene less than a year after the wedding.

Domestic daily life rushed over her like a wave, so much so that she still could not pinpoint when the change occurred, when Andrew slithered out from the shade of the grass.

Chapter 5
Kaifeck

Vika hesitated over seeing her neighbor, Lawrence Bauer, again. She had done a wonderful job of avoiding him since she returned. Theirs was a complicated relationship, and since she returned, their only encounters had taken place in a courtroom. She had known him as a young girl and confided far too much. He didn't keep her secret.

Lawrence had helped convict her father of unspeakable acts on the heels of her husband's death and the birth of her daughter, Celie. She refused to speak to him for well over a year. She felt so betrayed that this person, this one friend had taken the snapshot of her painful secrets that she had confessed in desperation and shouted them from the rooftops. She had never asked him why, afraid that his answer would make forgiving him completely impossible.

Today, he finally came to see her.

"Why, Vika Gruber, as I live and breathe." Lawrence Bauer strolled across the property to the stables where she was grooming the horses. Lawrence Bauer was the quintessential essence of tall and handsome (although fair-haired) …and married.

"Don't. Just don't, Lawrence," Vika replied.

"I'm sorry, Vika. I am so sorry. My intent never was to hurt you."

"Yet you did, Lawrence. You did hurt me, and betray my trust, and upset my entire life," she responded, trying to control the intensity of the brush on her horse as her anger increased.

"I was sorry to hear about your husband," Lawrence tried to steer the subject to something less volatile. "Viktoria still isn't doing so well." Viktoria was Lawrence's wife who had fallen ill earlier that year. Obviously, they were no longer waiting for her to recover.

Vika let the subject change, relieved to think about something else, "I'm so sorry, Lawrence. Is there anything I can do?" Lawrence grabbed a brush and started grooming Lightning, the next horse in the stable. For a moment, they both just groomed the horses in silence.

"Nothing to be done," he finally said quietly. It was weighing on him. She could tell. His wife was not getting better and it showed, without her even having to ask. His eyes were sunken in, with puffy skin holding his eyes like a cradle. He had lost weight. He couldn't afford that, as he was already a trim man. He was beginning to look gaunt. He was a man losing his wife, his love, and his purpose.

Lawrence and Vika had always been close. He was the only one who knew all of her secrets. If only he had kept them. He used to stroll by the farm when she was out tending to the cows. They would talk and laugh. She would, of course, ask after his wife. He was the one thing she had missed the most when she left the farm.

"I'm here now. I'm here for you," Vika offered and meant it.

"Thank you." Lawrence put down the brush and kissed her cheek, "I need to get back to Viktoria."

He took her by the shoulders and looked deep into her eyes, "Hear me, please. I never meant to hurt you." She knew it was the truth. Still, she could not forgive him for the pain and humiliation he put her through. She had trusted him.

He promised her he would make it right, and his only motivation was to protect her.

She promised him the abuse had stopped long ago and she was fine.

They both pretended to believe each other.

Chapter 6

"Father Traugott?" Vika entered the grand, long-standing, stone church, hoping to talk to her old pastor, "Father Traugott? You here?" She spotted him near the altar, replacing hymnals in the pews. "It's me, Vika Gabriel…um, Gruber."

He looked up, "Vika Gruber? As I live and breathe. Why, it's been so long, what, about two years?"

"Yes, Father."

"So good to see you, child." He embraced her fondly. They had grown close over the years and she still felt bad that she had never said goodbye when she wed.

"My husband, Karl, he was killed in the war. I recently moved back home to the farm with our baby daughter, Celie."

"I'm so sorry to hear about your husband, that war, such an awful thing," he replied, "But a baby, how wonderful! I cannot wait to meet the little angel."

"Thank you. I was hoping to rejoin the choir here at St. Vitus. I always loved singing here, some of my best memories are right here in this church. Are Alice and Sarah still here?" Alice, an elderly woman in the congregation, who had become like a mother to Vika and Sarah, a local schoolteacher, held a special place in Vika's heart. They had sung together in the choir for years, and neither of them was given the courtesy of a proper goodbye from Vika either. Vika was clearly horrible at goodbyes.

There was, of course, her other justification for waiving her formal goodbyes. One does not typically bring attention to oneself when running away. Father Traugott, Alice, Sarah – they all knew things were not right at the farm, and they also knew that Karl was far from the best choice for Vika. Given the choice, however, Karl was better than what she was being put through on the farm. It was a tough situation for all of them; they wanted the very best for Vika, but the very best did not present itself as a viable option for her. Vika felt the choice to ignore awkward goodbyes and just leave would be easier for everyone (let's be honest, especially herself). So, that was what she did.

"Of course, child. We would love to have you back. Oh, nothing would make me happier. Unless of course, you were to bring that precious baby to Mass with you next week?"

"I can definitely do that, Father. Thank you." She turned to leave.

"Vika?" Father Traugott called after her. She turned back. "I prayed for you every day. I still do." She smiled at the kind priest, feeling his concern, and perhaps a small sense of guilt for never stepping in. Why is it that such horrific acts can be so easily ignored in order to create a false sense of normalcy? Evil doesn't disappear just because people cover their eyes and wish it to go away. Yet, both of them still had their hands placed firmly over their eyes.

"Thank you, Father. See you next week." And with that, Vika quietly left the church and returned to the farm.

Chapter 7

Things had not been easy since the Great War, but it is amazing how adaptable people can become. The economy was in shambles and even the basics of potatoes, bread, and eggs cost a fortune. Vika's family had money and although they felt the pinch, they didn't feel it nearly like the majority of Bavarians who went to bed many nights with painfully empty stomachs. They were even further removed from those who were tragically even less fortunate, and starved to death. There appeared to be no hope of reprieve any time soon.

Vika also had to overcome being a single mother and a young widow. Honestly, that seemed to be easier for her to adapt to than moving home to the farm with her family. It was amazing what she could justify in order to have access to the security of regular food, shelter, and relative safety for her children. She was lying to herself and she knew it. As soon as the political and economic climate neutralized, she would go forward, on her own, with her daughter.

Kaifeck had seen more than its fair share of instability and it was not likely to stabilize anytime soon. Due to the reparations from the Great War that Germany had to repay, the economy continued its downward spiral. There seemed to be no upturn in sight.

Vika had once adored Ludwig II and believed in his devotion, not only to his Catholic faith, but also to his support of Germany during the Great War. His dedication to fair and balanced equality between Prussia and Bavaria encouraged her. She felt he had other choices, however, when he fled during the recent German Revolution. His people were starving and he didn't seem to care. He chose to save himself, his family, instead of his people. She felt personally betrayed by the Kaiser, whom she felt saved himself at the cost of his own people's lives. She was not sure what she thought of the premier Kurt Eisner and feared greatly for the future of Bavaria, but quietly hoped a new ruler would bring back hope and prosperity.

However, hope was all she did, like most people; the day-to-day demands of life were what she focused on. She had to maintain the farm and be a mother (and avoid her father). These were her duties right now. Political activism was not on her agenda. She had to do whatever was necessary for her and her daughter's survival right now. At least, for the moment, that meant returning to the farm and her family.

Vika rather quickly settled into a routine, working on the farm, singing in the choir at church, and trying to stay as invisible as possible.

Her mother had stayed rather quiet since her return, dutifully offering condolences on the loss of her husband and welcoming her and her baby daughter to the farm. Her father, on the other hand, let her know (in no uncertain terms) what an imposition this was for him, and what a great sacrifice he was making to allow her to come home. Once he was confident she felt ashamed and unwelcome, he ceased.

Chapter 8

Dietrich had kept mostly to himself since settling down in this small farming community up north. He sought employment at a local farm: harvesting, packaging, and hauling grain. It was decent money and arduous work, certainly not ideal, but good enough for now. It was a far cry from his dream career in banking, but the strenuous labor actually helped with his constant anxiety and worry that was such a plague to him. Each night, he collapsed in bed too exhausted to think. It was almost perfect.

Daylight haunted him less. Even on a very small scale, during the daytime hours, he was productive and needed, and that felt very good. It was once he was asleep that the trouble began. Every night, scenes flashed behind his eyelids. Images he was desperate to forget, but were such a part of him they were like an extra limb. Pictures from the Great War and Dietrich's last night in Munich fought for dominance behind his rapidly moving eyes. Tonight, the Great War won.

*****

I was alone in the middle of a bombed-out town, surrounded by bodies. Well, parts of bodies anyway. I was calling for my brother as soft, fat flakes of snow melted on my face.

Despite the bodies, it was quite serene, with the fluffy flakes of snow and the only sound – Christmas music. It escaping from the top floor of what, I can only assume, was the remains of an old apartment building. The sound was clear and unruffled, as whatever bombed the town had shattered the window glass.

"God rest ye merry gentlemen…"

I continued to shout for my brother as I made my way down the street, haphazardly pushing chunks of corpses out of my way as I trudged on.

Tis the season, I thought sardonically. "Hans!" I shouted out again. "Hans!"

"Hey, Dietrich! Buddy, over here!" A voice, loud and clear, called from behind me.

"Wait up! Why are you leaving me?" I recognized the voice of Little Mikey, one of the men from my platoon. I turned toward the voice as the figure rapidly filled the space between us, as if on some invisible pulley. "Hey man, wait up." I tried to comprehend what I was looking at. Mikey's jaw hung, swinging easily, from the right side of his face. As he moved, it appeared as if it was trying to flag me down.

How the hell can he talk? I thought. Ah, the beauty of dreams.

He continued rapidly forward until he was directly in front of me. His voice was still clear despite the state of his face. It was the most twisted ventriloquist act I had ever seen.

"Why'd you let them get me, man?" You said you'd look out for me." I was transfixed by the left side of his head, where (I am not a medical professional, so this is only a guess) his frontal lobe was exposed. While carrion beetles nibbled away at the gray meat, maggots crawled in and out of what remained. Mikey didn't seem to notice or mind. My gaze fell down a bit. The snow was still fluffy and falling; I watched it fall onto his tongue and dissolve, briefly reminding me of childhood, then instantly bringing me back to the fact that Mikey's tongue was bloated and black, and lying flat against his neck.

I stuttered. I don't remember ever doing that before, but apparently, *Dream Dietrich* catches a stutter when scared completely shitless. "I…I'm ssss…sss…sorry, Mikey. I'm sorry."

Little Mikey swung his arm around and punched me in the shoulder. The force sent his loose jaw swinging rapidly again. "Aww. It's okay, buddy. Got a smoke?"

"Oh, tidings of comfort and joy, comfort and joy…"

I screamed.

*****

Dietrich woke up in his bed, soaking wet; screaming in real life too. Looking at the clock, he saw he still had two hours before work. That was fine, he wasn't going back to sleep anytime soon, maybe never. He flung the damp sheets off his legs and got out of bed. He guessed he would be going into work early today. He was eager to let the strenuous monotony of his job free him from the monsters in his mind for a while.

Chapter 9

What was meant to be a temporary fix had silently turned into a semi-permanent solution. Vika still spoke of leaving the farm and getting away (even out of Germany, altogether) with Celie, but nothing ever materialized. No actual steps were taken. Vika had been eased back into the comfort of something familiar, even the worst of situations can become tolerable when one becomes accustomed to them. Vika had once again begun to justify her father's actions, which shamed her incredibly. With the shame came self-doubt, which in turn made her even more susceptible to her father's lies and her own justification. More shame + more justification = no movement.

Yet, as broken as she was, Vika had a heart, a beautiful heart. And even in this situation, she was a good mother. She wouldn't allow anybody to hurt her little girl. She may be able to wish away her own suffering, but she knew her heart would never be able to do the same if the suffering belonged to Celie.

"Get that ratty thing off the table, Celie," Father spoke up during breakfast. "Since your mother hasn't done it, I'll get you a new doll, a better one, and we can throw that one away."

Dealing with Father's criticisms was a regular part of life now and Vika hardly noticed anymore. It was amazing what became tolerable when it was necessary.

"Nooooo, Grandpappy," Celie hid Muffin's raggedy body under the table, "Muffin's family."

"She's a doll!" he raised his voice, "And she's dirty and falling apart. For Pete's sake, she only has one eye!"

He was right. Muffin was painfully worn. Her once brilliant cloth body and face were gray from being dragged everywhere with Celie since she was a baby. Her calico dress was dirty and proudly sported a raspberry jam stain right in the middle, like a gunshot wound. Muffin only had four yarn strings of hair left on her head, but Celie smoothed them with loving care every night as she went to sleep. Celie loved her, just her, as she was. She had no desire for a new doll.

Celie started to cry. Vika attempted to placate the situation, "Baby, maybe Momma can fix her up a bit. Hand wash her? Make her a new dress?" Vika placed her hand on Celie's leg under the table to silently let her know she wouldn't allow Muffin to go anywhere. It stopped the crying.

"You can't shine shit, Vika," Father interrupted. "I'll never understand you." He glanced at Celie, "Either of you."

He seemed to give up and went back to eating his eggs.

He was right. He would never understand. One cannot explain love to someone who has never felt it.

Chapter 10

Other than motherhood, Vika's only other opportunity for contentment in her life was at church. The people, the music, the friendships she developed, were so cherished. The church was the one place where the whispers and judgmental stares didn't follow, and she was so very grateful for that.

The truth was Pastor Traugott, Alice, and Sarah took the time to get to know Vika. They loved her for who she was, not what she had done. It was a warm and welcome relief every Wednesday when she came to town for choir practice.

Each Wednesday, Vika left Celie in Zenzi's care and confidently walked to the church in town. Celie loved the Gruber's maid and enjoyed the time she had with her on Wednesdays, playing and helping with chores. Much like her mother, Celie found joy in little, simple things.

Vika always knew Zenzi was a little jealous of her. Perhaps it was how close in age they were, or Vika's sudden return home, either way, Vika did her best to get along. They couldn't be considered friends, but Vika respected her and trusted her with her daughter when she wasn't there.

Chapter 11

It had been some months since Lawrence's wife passed on. Vika had seen him once or twice since then, but his visits had ceased recently. Vika knew exactly why and was desperate to make things right.

Things had crossed the line. He had been grieving and lonely, and kissed her passionately as she comforted him. She did not resist. She should have, but she was just as lonely and had missed so much the feeling of being wanted. They both knew it was a mistake and cut things off as quickly as they started, but his hasty and awkward retreat on that day proved his regret.

Vika just wished he would return so she could tell him that she agreed they should forget the whole thing ever happened. However, that chance wouldn't come if he never came by again.

Lawrence had really become a genuine friend to her since her return. Their friendship had grown and matured. Other than Pastor Traugott, Alice, and Sarah, she had no friends and no romantic interests – or time for them. Vika did not want to lose the one confidant she held dear to her. He was safe, comfortable, and she missed him.

They had passed on the street in town a couple of times, but nothing was exchanged except a courteous nod. It seemed a bit extreme to her. They were adults after all. It hardly garnered this amount of punishment. And, after all, he was the one who kissed her. Why was she feeling like the one who should be ashamed?

Today, she would end it. She would march right over to him and insist they forget all about this ridiculousness and put it behind them. Confident within her resolve, she readied herself as she saw him begin to exit Café Brotgarten. She crossed the street with quick, determined steps, stopping suddenly on the sidewalk near the café. Lawrence had lingered in the doorway, waiting to take the hand of a pretty brunette woman. He led her, arm-in-arm, down the street in the opposite direction.

Vika sighed, defeated. Maybe this was the end of their friendship.

Chapter 12
Andrew and Cas, 1888

Cas and Andrew had never been what anyone would call affectionate. Andrew was a man's man. Nevertheless, the little things he did during their short courtship disappeared one by one. He no longer held her hand in public, or at all. He did not compliment her hair or dress, even when she put obvious effort into her appearance. His kiss was no longer tender. He was harsh, demanding, and unapologetic when he needed her to perform her marital duties. *This is what it is to be a woman,* Cas thought to herself. *This is marriage.*

She found some worth in her children, although she never had that natural maternal instinct all mothers were supposed to have inside them. This frustrated her to no end. She didn't have it with her older children, and definitely not with little Victoria, her only living child from Andrew.

Victoria was such an easy baby. She hardly cried at all, slept through the night, and was easy to entertain. Cas' heart should have swelled with maternal nurturing and love, but it did not. Instead, she resented the small amount of attention that Andrew showed the baby. He was thrilled he had a daughter, and although he did nothing to help take care of her, he gave her the affection, the hugs, and kisses Cas wanted for herself. God forgive her, she was jealous of her child.

Cas prayed to outgrow this insecurity about her own daughter, to develop the nurturing soul she knew she should have, but day after day, as Viktoria grew, nothing changed inside of Cas. No compassion developed for her child. No protective instinct came. No unique feelings at all, if she was to be completely honest. Well, that's not completely true, the jealousy and resentment increased with every passing day.

Viktoria developed into a beautiful young woman and Cas noticed a shift in her husband's attention toward their daughter, an unnatural shift that was unthinkable to Cas. It was inconceivable.

So, Cas looked the other way; she ignored it. She disregarded her daughter's tears and moods as adolescent growing pains. After some time, she easily believed in the reality she created. She fell into an oblivious comfort in her life, as her daughter continued to fight her demons alone.

The only thing that pulled Cas back into the truth of the atrocities under her roof was being around Vika too much. To combat this, Cas became more reserved and withdrawn from her daughter; treating her more like a hired hand than her child. It benefitted Cas in two ways: first, she could live her life in ignorance and relative peace, secondly, she felt more comfortable with this distance between Vika and her, it seemed more natural. So much so, that she no longer bothered herself with any sense of guilt over not being maternal. It just didn't seem to matter anymore.

Chapter 13
Kaifeck

It took a few months, but Lawrence eventually returned. Vika was thrilled; she had sincerely missed him. He knew her better than anyone and still desired to be her friend. He still saw the good in her and that meant everything, especially since she so rarely recognized it in herself.

"Hi, Vika, need some help with the cattle?" Lawrence walked up hesitantly and offered a hand and smiling down at Celie, who was hiding behind her momma's skirt.

"No, I'm fine, thanks." Now that he was here, she wasn't certain she wanted to make this easy for him.

"Wow, Miss Celie, you have grown so big since I last saw you!" Lawrence continued, running his fingers through his sandy locks nervously. The little girl began to come out from behind her mother, "I'm almost five years old now."

Lawrence looked back up at Vika, "It has been too long. I'm sorry."

"Celie, honey, why don't you go inside and help Grandmother and Zenzi prepare for dinner?" This was more of a directive than a request. Either way, the little girl reached up, grasping her mother's cheeks in her tiny palms, giving her a kiss, before running off to the main house.

As the little girl disappeared inside, Vika turned to Lawrence, "I am so sorry too. I should never have let anything happen. I am so embarrassed." All pretense of making this difficult for him vanished. Vika was so relieved to have her friend back. She really needed him right now.

He shook his head, "Nonsense, I am fully responsible. Let's just put it behind us."

"Yes," Vika breathed out deeply. "Friends?"

"Absolutely. I…" He wanted to ask something; she could tell.

She immediately countered; weary of what he would say next, changing the subject, "Did you hear? Eisner was assassinated in Munich."

"It's all anyone can talk about."

"It is speculated that Hoffmann, the Minister of Education, will take his place."

"Germany needs a break. Our people are miserable. Maybe this new change will help put food back on our tables."

"Agreed. I hope this latest turn of events can make our futures just a bit brighter. Even in our positions, it is causing worry. Our marks are practically worthless and are worth even less almost daily. Still, we are better off than most of Germany."

Noticing his pat answers to her and the strain on his face, she knew he was not deterred. "What is it?"

Lawrence looked her directly in the eyes and took a deep breath. Reaching out, he took both her hands tightly in his, not detracting his gaze, he began, "Well, I have heard whispers around town." His gaze now absently went to her protruding stomach.

Her head fell. She wasn't ready to lose him again already.

"You told me it stopped."

Refusing to look at him, she turned away, shame swallowing her in a suffocating wave. She admitted the truth, "I can't stop him." She burst into tears. If he was going to be lost forever, he should know it all.

Looking around conspiratorially and seeing that nobody was around, she dragged him over to the side of the barn and painfully told him everything. She told him the rest, all of the things she had previously vowed to take to her grave: how it began, the unnerving terror she would feel when she saw the light break through the crack in her bedroom door, illuminating his figure in the hallway: her ten-year-old body faking sleep, curling herself into a protective ball. Andrew, trying to convince her it was natural and that she wanted it just as much as he did, then, when that failed, how it escalated to threats to her mother, to herself, if she ever spoke a word of it. How her eventual escape to Karl only changed the role of the villain in her nightmare, but not the horror; and even now, her fear of where his derelictions would lead him if she refused to comply.

Something took hold of her and all her secrets came to the surface, each word opening the wound, yet shedding a healing light on it at the same time. When she was finished, she dared to look him in the eyes. Her tears were now dry; his horror apparent, but he didn't leave. Instead, he shed tears of his own and held her. When he tilted her head up toward his, she wasn't sure what to expect. She certainly did not expect what came out of his mouth next.

Lawrence grabbed both her hands tightly in his, "My dear friend, I have a plan."

Chapter 14

It had been over a year now and there was one thing Dietrich still needed to do. For some reason, he had been so reluctant to make this move, but he felt the void almost physically, and he knew it was time.

He hadn't entered a church in so long, yet as he pulled the strong wooden doors open, he had to admit he had missed it. St. Vitus; it was the closest church to his small flat in town. As he walked down the center aisle, he felt a comforting familiarity blended with the uneasy sense of being an outsider, a fraud.

Dietrich genuflected naturally, crossed himself, and scooted into the closest pew to kneel down. His eyes closed; he regulated his breathing; he was attempting to just be in the moment with God. He had just achieved this when a hand on his shoulder made him jump.

"Forgive me, son. I didn't mean to startle you." The old priest let go of Dietrich's shoulder and offered him his hand, "I'm Father Traugott. I'm the pastor here at St. Vitus."

Dietrich sat back in his pew and strained to find words. "I haven't been to your parish before," he started, "In fact, I haven't been to any church in quite some time." Fr. Traugott smiled kindly in response.

"Well, I am so grateful you came today, Mr...."

"Praeter. Dietrich Praeter."

"Mr. Praeter, it was a pleasure to meet you. I'll allow you to return to your prayers." Father Traugott began to walk away, then stopped, and looked back to address him again, "If you'd like to talk when you are finished, I'll be right over here." Again, he flashed that kindly smile. This priest made him feel immediately welcome. Dietrich knelt back down and began to pray, feeling much more confident in his return, and thanking God for the warm welcome.

Chapter 15

Vika's pregnancy was never discussed on the farm, at least not among the adults. Celie and she discussed it, of course, but Celie's excitement for a baby brother or sister was instinctually contained around others. But alone with Vika, she exploded with eager excitement, "Momma, Momma, Momma, let me touch my baby!" Vika giggled. Celie's delight was intoxicating.

"Okay, okay, Celie." Vika pushed down the quilt that covered them on the old brass bed and lifted her nightgown to expose her rapidly growing belly.

"It's beautiful!" she cried with a child's sincerity, as she wrapped her little arms around Vika's bump and laid her head on it.

"You're beautiful, Buttercup," Vika smiled down at Celie's exuberant face and stroked her pale hair. Celie, in turn, began doing the same to her doll, Muffin.

Suddenly, Celie shot up, with a look of seriousness on her cherubic face. "Now, a baby is a lot of responsibility. (It was nice to know she listened when Vika spoke to her.)" Vika instantly met her seriousness and leaned in to learn more.

"Go on."

"Well, I will help with EVERYTHING." She opened her arms around her as wide as they would go, "I will feed the baby. Rock the baby. Ch…" she stopped suddenly, "Play with the baby."

Vika laughed aloud, "Well, you will be the best big sister ever, won't you?" She pulled the little girl onto her lap, while there was still room, "I love you so much, Buttercup. You are my whole heart."

"The baby too?"

"Oh yes, the baby too."

"How can we both be your whole heart?"

"Well, it's the magic of being a mommy. My heart, it just keeps growing to make room for you both."

Celie sat up with wide eyes and concern etched on her face, "Momma, you can love me a little less if you need to."

Vika looked puzzled, "Why, Buttercup?"

"I don't think you can grow much bigger than you are now!"

Chapter 16

Dietrich couldn't believe he was thirty-seven years old today. He celebrated alone in his flat with a pint of Hops and a Lucky Strike. That was fine by him. He was getting used to his solitary existence. Sure, he got lonely, but people were complicated, and loving them took effort and caused hurt. There was too much risk involved. Besides, with all the ghosts he already had in his life, Dietrich had all the company he could handle.

He leaned back and stretched out the length of his bed, closing his eyes and inhaling another deep toke of the cigarette. He thought back to when his life was relatively easy with Hans. He missed him so much that he felt it physically. He remembered laughter and genuine love between them. Joy filled the gaps between the arguments and growing pains that came along with one brother raising the other. No matter how angry one of them got with the other, they always came back together. That was before Hans became someone Dietrich didn't recognize. From then on, with Hans, there was no longer room for compromise. Any discussion was beset by corrosive ideology that nothing short of an exorcism could relieve. Dietrich knew his only option, at this point, was to forge ahead with his life in Kaifeck. His future was here now.

Chapter 17

"Celie, Celie, baby," Vika called out in halted gasps. Of all the times to be completely alone, the only person she could see was Celie, playing with Muffin by the side of the barn. Vika took in as much breath as she could and tried her best to shout, "Celie, Mommy needs you!" She saw her little girl's head pop up and look in her direction. Thank God, she heard her.

Bracing her hands on her thighs, Vika bore down in spite of herself, as she waited for Celie to come to her.

Celie ran up to her, stopping suddenly, "Momma, you had an accident," looking down at the puddle of water between her mother's legs, "Big girls don't have accidents. You told me that."

"Celie, listen carefully, the baby is coming now. Run fast and get Zenzi and Grandmother. I don't think I can get inside on my own."

Celie's eyes grew wide with excitement, "Okay, okay, Momma; I'll bring them right back." She continued to shout over her shoulder as she ran to the house.

Moments later, Vika's mother and Zenzi came running out, flanking her on either side. Lifting Vika's arms over each of their shoulders, they rushed her inside the house to her bedroom.

Did it hurt this badly with Celie? Vika tried to recall as the waves of excruciating pain took her breath away. During the intermittent releases from pain, she tried to convince herself that she wasn't really in labor yet. She was fine. It was just gas. Her mother eased her onto the bed and helped her out of her shoes, stockings, and underclothes. Cas then left to get a bowl of cool water and a cloth.

She wiped her brow as Zenzi stayed, prepared at the end of the bed. The alternate cooling from the damp cloth and the intense pain of the contractions seemed to alternate endlessly. Hours passed and in a momentary reprieve from pain, Vika allowed brief sleep to overtake her exhausted body.

"Okay, Vika, push. It's time." The clenching pain in her abdomen coupled with Zenzi's demands stirred her to consciousness, "Vika, come on and push!"

She bore down with every bit of strength she possessed. Not enough.

"Again," Zenzi shouted.

"You do it!" she sassed back. How had she gone through this before and survived? She didn't remember it hurting this much. She collapsed back onto the bed.

"Come on." Cas lifted her back up to a sitting position.

"Push again," Zenzi repeated.

"Again, again," Vika mimicked, as she realized this was going to happen with or without her permission. "I…can't…do…this!" Vika screamed, as she pushed with an effort she did not know she had.

This time, when Vika collapsed back on the bed, they let her stay there. The air was punctuated with a high-pitched cry.

I did do it, Vika thought.

"It's a boy," Zenzi announced. His cries rivaled hers.

"I want him," Vika panted.

"Let me clean him up." Zenzi took him to the other side of the room where she had clean towels and fresh water waiting. Celie peeked in, waiting anxiously at the door.

"Okay, Celie," Cas called out to her, as Zenzi handed the new little bundle to Vika, "You can come in and meet your baby brother."

"A brother!" she squealed, as she darted toward the bed.

"Gentle!" Zenzi admonished, "Your mother is fragile right now, and so is the baby. Vika was heartened with this rare showing of compassion from Zenzi.

"Thank you, Zenzi, for everything."

Zenzi simply nodded in reply and continued cleaning up. Celie scooted carefully onto the bed, "Momma, he's all squishy and red. Did you do it wrong?"

"No, Buttercup," she laughed, "All new babies look that way at first. He'll change. You'll see."

"You are his kangaroo," Celie smiled, "We learned all about them in school. The mommies carry the babies in their pockets, right here," she said, patting Vika's belly, "He's your baby Joey!"

"I like it," Vika replied, looking down at her son, "Hello, baby Joey."

Chapter 18

Vika was actually allowed into town by herself more often after little Joey was born, not out of Andrew's kindness, of course, but because he felt her state as a single, new mother (and the figure to prove it) would be enough to keep any potential suitors away.

She couldn't even relish the freedom. She was too busy trying to ignore the stares and whispers that came from every direction; dodging the torment of passive-aggressive judgement.

There was still an expected shame when a woman had a child out of wedlock. It was not unspoken, quite the contrary. It was spoken of constantly and with great, excited fervor. It was whispered behind you as you left the post office. It was embedded in scolding glances and scathing glares that spoke volumes at the general store.

This was almost preferable to the direct, unabashed judgement that came from those who used you as a cautionary tale to scare their children into compliance.

However, all of the above, the speculation, the judgement, that she was a loose woman who whored around with a weak widower, was preferable to the truth.

"He couldn't help himself."

"He was grieving his lost love."

"She bewitched him."

This was so much more desirable than the deep-rooted shame of the other gossip; the other words, that hovered in the minds and on the lips of so many.

"You know, she is screwing her father."

Chapter 19

It still seemed unreal to her. Lawrence had risked his reputation, his business, and his future relationships, on a lie, on her lie. When he had proposed the idea to float the rumor that he fathered her baby, she was shocked.

Lawrence did ask for something in return. She had to get on her feet and away from the farm. He was giving her a way out of public scandal and she agreed to get away from the sickness of her father once and for all.

There, of course, was still the misogynistic, societal double standard. In reality, Lawrence's reputation hardly took a hit. And, even though many bought the lie, Vika was still shunned, scolded, talked about, and ignored by most of those in town. Whatever the story, she was to blame; after all, (in the words of her mother) she was a woman.

However, people lose interest after a while and some other poor soul's problems become the 'new scandal.' Vika could live with the stares and whispers; all she had to do was look at that beautiful, innocent baby. He had no idea how he got here, he was just so happy to be here, and she loved him so completely and separate from his conception.

She had just come back from the post office and market with the children. She heard the screaming well before she came to the front door to the house.

"Celie, honey, why don't you take Joey to the barn and play with Barney for a few minutes. I will send Zenzi to get you in a few minutes. Okay?"

"Okay, Momma." Celie stood on her tiptoes to give Vika a kiss, then took her baby brother and headed away from the house to go play with her cherished dog. She was only a child, but she understood what was going on.

Vika steadied herself and entered the house.

"How hard is it to make a decent potato salad, Cas? Can you explain this to me?" Andrew pushed the bowl of potato salad in her mother's face.

"You are a German woman for hell's sake, how can you not know how to make potato salad?" Her mother had been backed up until she hit the counter, and now just cowered as he berated her.

"Hi," Vika announced loudly. It was worth a try, maybe he would back down. Also, it was the only idea she had right now.

He looked at Vika with disgust and frustration, and then threw the full bowl of potato salad in the sink next to her mother. "Make something else," he spat at her and then turned to Vika, as he left, "Help your mother with dinner. She needs it."

"So, potato salad, huh," Vika walked over to her mother and gave her a half hug, "It's okay. We'll make sausage and mash. It's his favorite." Cas nodded at her daughter gratefully and began to gather what they needed to begin cooking.

"He should appreciate you more," Vika started, without looking at her mom, as they peeled potatoes at the sink.

"Don't start, Victoria. You don't know what it is like to be a wife."

"Mom, I was married."

"Not long. Not long enough to know that there are many ways women suffer in marriage. It is just the way it is."

"Really? Is it? I'm starting to think, maybe, women aren't supposed to be miserable in their marriages, maybe we both just married ass…"

"Victoria, enough!" I will not have you speak of your father that way in this house!"

Vika had no verbal response; the insanity of this conversation left her speechless. She just continued with dinner preparation in silence. Inside, she was seething, not with her mother, but herself and her own ridiculous pretense. What a hypocrite she was. She tolerated her father's abuse, first out of fear, then out of shame. She bore Karl's beatings and infidelity, and probably would be still, if he were alive. She was just like her mother, and the realization made her physically ill.

Vika's feeble attempts to normalize her family situation were foolish. There was no way she could pretend enough, help enough, smile enough, or look the other way enough to make staying here at the farm any longer okay. Nothing here was okay or normal; it was sick, and when she was here, she was part of the sickness too. She rushed from the house and around the side, purging the contents of her stomach. If she did not make a change now, she would drag her beloved Celie into this cycle of self-deprecating torment and exploitation. Her realization had properly chastised her, she would either continue to be the very thing she detested, or change now. She would change. However, undoing a lifetime of sickness was easier said than done, and Vika truly had no idea where to begin.

Chapter 20

Dietrich walked to work, examining the faces of the men and women he passed. He wondered if underneath the put-together exteriors, the tailored suits and smiling facades, did they, too, feel like children dressing up in their parents' clothes playing pretend, just waiting for someone to call their bluff as they fumbled through their daily routine pretending to be an adult? He sure as hell hoped he was not alone in this. He pulled the collar of his coat up to ward off the chilled air as he walked. He hoped that magical age, where one came 'into-their-own' and their skin fit comfortably, arrived soon.

With all of the adult responsibilities Dietrich had thrust upon him in his life, one would think he was a very comfortable adult. He honestly did not know if he would ever feel as if he knew what he was doing. Acting like an adult and feeling like an adult were two very different accomplishments. Wouldn't it be strange if everyone walked around feeling like this, but were too embarrassed to say so?

Dietrich ducked into Kaiser's grocery to pick up this week's *Munich News-Kourier*. This was the only place in Kaifeck that carried it (it wasn't terribly popular), but it allowed him to keep tabs on what was going on back home, and hopefully, give him some piece of mind about where he left his little brother.

He read the headlines twice. Political tension was on the rise. Things were definitely going in a wrong direction. How can people support these ideas? Or the real question he had, how can Hans? Each week, he saw a headline like this, and wondered how it could get any worse; people cannot get any worse. Oh, but it does, and they do. People never cease to prove there is a lower level to reach.

Dietrich imagined, foolhardily, that Hans was far too busy keeping the bakery going without him, to spend any time pursuing his political interest, that he was no longer involved with these people. Dietrich prayed, he hoped, and he knew better.

Chapter 21

"How's my little man?" Lawrence picked Joey up and held him high to look at him. Currently, giggling and drooling topped the list of new skills.

"You're very good with him," Vika softly commented from the kitchen table, where she sat peeling potatoes.

He sat across from Vika with the baby happily on his lap, "I love him, Vika." He was quiet until she was forced to look up at him. He held her eyes with his. His message was clear and final, "I am his father."

Vika smiled. Smiled and started to cry. That was sort of her thing ever since having Joey. Her emotions were raw and unedited – All. The. Time. "I know. Thank you."

"Okay then," he started, as he stood and crossed over to hand her the baby. "Enough of this," he wiped her cheek with the back of his calloused hand. He kissed Joey on his head before leaving to return to work.

Lawrence was a frequent part of Joey's life, but not vital to it. He did not shy away from the two of them in public and visited, although briefly, often. Vika finally became more comfortable with this overly generous and selfless act of his. Rumors still swirled, but now, he had created an even more viable alternative to explain her beautiful boy's disturbing conception.

Nothing stays unchanged forever, though, no matter how much she desired it to do so. Times change, so does situations and people, and as much as Lawrence loved them, he was also a strong, healthy man. So, of course, as Lawrence began to date again, as was expected, he had Vika's full support. She had to admit, she was a wee bit jealous, not romantically, of course, but because she wished somewhere, quietly inside, for the same fortune for herself.

As of late, a woman named Anna had been a constant presence with Lawrence when Vika would see him in town. They would hold hands as they walked down the avenue. She would playfully touch his arm and laugh adoringly when he spoke. Things seemed to be getting serious very quickly.

Vika hadn't broached the subject with Lawrence for fear of affecting their current pretense of parental bliss. She hoped to hold onto this as long as she possibly could.

Vika had nothing against Anna. She was a pretty, soft-spoken brunette, about which nobody seemed to have anything bad to say. Her stomach clenched nonetheless. Vika knew as difficult as it would be for her, if Lawrence left, she would survive. It wasn't for her that her stomach turned in knots. It was for Joey. Anna had a son of her own, an eight-year-old, ironically named Joey. Vika's Joey lit up around Lawrence. He recognized him and even called him 'Papa.' Vika let out a silent prayer, in hope Lawrence would not be eased out of Joey's life all together.

Chapter 22

Life was getting better, Vika thought. Celie had just turned six and started school down the road, while Joey was getting more animated by the day. He was about to turn a year old in a few weeks. Time was flying, and as long as she focused on her kids, Vika was happy and was able to put her worries about Lawrence out of her mind. She was already looking into plans to move away with the children. She knew, somehow, she would leave her father's farm very soon. Nothing had actually changed at the farm, but her clarity about it had made a huge difference in her. She felt renewed, focused. She had regained a speck of hope.

Of course, she had her Wednesday escapes to church to sing with her friends. She was practically skipping on her way there today.

Vika pulled open the heavy French doors of St. Vitus and stopped in her tracks. Choir practice had a decidedly different air this week. Some handsome sandy-haired stranger was talking with Pastor Traugott.

Vika entered the sanctuary and just stared for a moment. Either she had been alone for way too long, or this was the best-looking man she had ever seen. He was moderately tall. Not towering, like Lawrence, but tiptoes to kiss height – perfect. He was ruggedly built, not stocky, but visibly muscular under his brown-tweed suit. He was no stranger to hard work; that was certain. Not much status in that, but then again, Vika had never been one to pay attention to the social status of others, despite her upbringing.

He glanced in her direction, halted his expression for a moment, and then smiled. Her stomach flipped so that she placed her hands instinctively over it to halt the movement. He had an amazing smile that transformed his face, ending in dimples that somehow fit perfectly with his strong, square jawline.

She smiled back (or so she thought), the result was a grimace, typically reflective of intestinal issues. His smile disappeared. The more she tried to morph her expression into a natural smile, the more unnatural it felt – as revealed in Mr. Handsome's face. His bright smile faded to a look of...concern. She tried to steady herself casually against the doorframe but missed it by a hair. Her grimace was now genuine as she fell to the floor in a tangled heap. *Dammit! Ouch.*

Suddenly, Father Traugott and Mr. Handsome were assisting her off the floor. "Are you okay?" the gorgeous stranger asked.

"Good. Good," she replied, as she smoothed out her skirt over her black stockings.

"Good. Thank you." Perhaps pure repetition would make it believable. "And you?" she countered. Let's make this normal. This will be the new normal for socializing. This will now be how normal conversations begin.

He looked puzzled. Vika kept her face dedicated to the normalcy of this exchange. Her head, cocked to the side, an inquisitive look: *I'm great, now really, how are you?*

"I'm, uh, I'm doing well. Thanks." He stood back and stuck out his hand, "I am Dietrich Praeter. I moved up here from Munich. And you are?"

"Vika, Vika Gruber. I sing here with the choir." His hand was strong and surprisingly smooth.

"Well, Vika Gruber, who sings with the choir, it is an absolute pleasure to meet you. I look forward to seeing you again soon." He tipped his hat and breezed past her and out of the church. Vika didn't even realize she was standing as still as a statue, reflecting on this encounter, until Fr. Traugott leaned in and whispered, "Breathe, Child," with a small, amused grin on his face, "Let's start practice."

Chapter 23

Dear Mother of God, what was wrong with her? Vika replayed the interaction with the amazingly handsome and forever horrified Mr. Praeter at church. Was there a mental issue? Did she need to be committed? Was she clearly unsafe to interact with people at large? Vika was convinced her mere moments with the stranger had caused him to flee back to Munich in terror. *I will probably never see him again,* she thought, somewhat comforted, but also saddened by the thought. He was so good-looking and he seemed genuinely nice, and he was Catholic, he had to be, why else would he be at the church talking to Father Traugott. Vika got lost in imagining a large church wedding...

"A mark for your thoughts?" Sarah slid into the pew beside her.

"Oh no, it is worth much more than that to keep them to myself," Vika replied with a wink.

The perky, young schoolteacher guessed anyway, "It wouldn't have anything to do with the handsome new parishioner Father Traugott was talking to before practice, would it?"

Vika blushed involuntarily. "Of course not," she tried to sound indignant. "Absolutely not. No...yes. Yes, it does. He's so cute," she gushed.

Sarah laughed.

"Listen to me, I sound like a schoolgirl. I am in my thirties. I'm a mother," Vika sighed heavily, "I am so embarrassed."

"Don't be. He is quite handsome," Sarah whispered conspiratorially.

Vika looked at her married, pregnant friend in mock shock.

"It's an observation, that's all," Sarah added, "I may have observed something else too." She glanced sideways at her friend, "But I'm sure you wouldn't be interested."

"Tell me, tell me, tell me," Vika pleaded in a similar fashion as her daughter might.

"I may have overheard that our little choir is getting another alto."

Nausea and excitement filled Vika's body. "Until next week then," she replied, suppressing a grin.

Chapter 24

The next Wednesday took forever to arrive, and even though Vika had repeated to herself a million times over that Mr. Praeter was probably back in Munich and wouldn't even be there, she took extra care in getting ready that morning, even trading her thick black stockings for a more stylish, polished knee-high boot.

She admonished herself, even as she applied a touch of rouge to her cheeks. She had more important things on which to focus right now. She was a mother; she had no time for dating. Still, the thought of that handsome stranger had kept visiting her mind regularly throughout the entire week.

She was giddy. *Gross. Come on, you are a grown woman, Vika!* She silently admonished herself. She was regaining focus, looking toward a happy, independent future with her children. A romance was too complicated to interject in her life right now. Still…

Chapter 25

It had been a few weeks since Dietrich joined the choir. He wanted to become more involved with his new parish, but of course, seeing the lovely Vika Gruber at practice each week was a nice benefit. They had begun to talk a bit before and after practices. He learned she was a widowed mother of two, and lived with her parents on their farm just outside of town. With each passing day, he began to accept his current life as his only life: his only reminder – the Munich newspaper. Dietrich still purchased one every Sunday to check up on those still there, especially his brother. He would search for familiar names in the crimes and obituary sections. Hoping not to find any, and then basking in relief on those weeks he did not.

This week, he basked. And he sat next to the enchanting Vika as everyone left practice.

"So what brought you here from Munich?" Vika asked him, as they sat in an empty pew after practice.

"It's a long story. I'm sure you don't have time for it."

"I do. I want to hear it, and I have all the time in the world today. Since Father Traugott isn't feeling well and cut practice short, my father isn't expecting me back for a couple of hours still." She smiled coyly, "Plenty of time for an interesting story."

Dietrich chuckled, "I said long, not interesting."

"I guess I better be the judge of that. I bet it's a dilly!"

He had no intention of sharing any part of his past. What was it about this woman that made him want to? He took a deep breath. He was so tired of playing it safe. *What the hell, I could always move again.* "Alright then, you asked for it. I was born and raised in Munich. Both of my parents grew up there, met in school, married and stayed to raise a family. I never really thought of going anywhere else."

"Do you have any siblings?" She seemed to be checking standard questions off some sort of list in her mind.

"Yes. I have a younger brother, Hans. He's twelve years my junior. My mother had three miscarriages between Hans and me. My parents really didn't think she could carry any more children. Then, surprise! Here comes Hans. He's actually the reason I stayed there as long as I did." He chuckled slightly to himself, "Why am I telling you all of this?"

She smiled in return, "I am so glad you are. Go on. What about your parents, are they still there?"

"They died when I was twenty-six. A car accident while vacationing in Paris," Dietrich closed his eyes at the memory, "It was the first time they had ever taken a vacation together, just the two of them. They had saved for three years."

She reached out and touched his leg, "I am so sorry, Dietrich."

He grabbed her hand, "I am always sad that they are gone. That never goes away, but more than that, if I'm really truthful, I'm angry; so angry, that they worked so hard to – get to die." She sat quietly, waiting for him to go on, or stop. He didn't know. He was just grateful she gave him a moment to reflect on his loss. He was shocked at the amount he was willingly sharing with this virtual stranger, yet he was equally as surprised at how natural it seemed to do so.

He took a breath and patted her hand to let her know he was ready to continue, "So, here I was twenty-six years old and raising a fourteen-year-old kid."

"That had to be so hard. You are so strong."

"No, don't look at me like that. I wasn't a hero. My brother and I always got on well, and we had wonderful neighbors. They helped when they could. It wasn't that bad." Dietrich thought of one neighbor, in particular, he had passed his obituary in the paper the week after he left. He was devastated, but not surprised. He knew how he died, and the paper lied. He snapped back to the present. He was definitely not sharing that, not even with her.

"Anyway, I was working at Munich Bank and had to leave so I could come home and take care of Hans and run my papa's bakery."

"Bakery, yum." She broke the seriousness of their talk with a playful nudge of her shoulder, "A man that can bake."

"I can, yes. If you are lucky, I will make you our famous Apple Strudel. We had people come from all around for our family recipe." He smiled back at her. Wow, she had beautiful eyes. Sometimes, just a look can feel like a touch. Close, private, the kind that makes your breath catch in your throat.

Dietrich could tell the moment was a little too intimate for her. "Well, good, I look forward to it," she looked away, busying herself with smoothing out her skirt, "Why don't we start the next chapter of the Dietrich sagas next week? I should be getting home."

"Okay," he responded.

Vika got up and walked toward the grand double doors of St. Vitus. Turning back, she addressed him once more, "Thank you."

"For what?"

"Sharing yourself with me. It was…nice hearing about where you came from. I look forward to learning more about you." With that, she turned to go, leaving him alone in the church.

Chapter 26
Munich, 1908

I was attacked with a seemingly never-ending succession of hugs, firm handshakes, and sympathetic pats on the back; surrounded by a fog of 'too soon,' 'Dietrich, they were such dear people,' and, 'you poor boys.'

Just stop! I wanted to scream, but instead, I stood beside my parents' coffins and smiled graciously, thanking each fuzzy face that offered their condolences. My senses were assaulted with incense, a menagerie of perfume scents, and my own sweat. The church was stifling today.

Hans stood to my right, crying unashamedly; he simply could not contain his grief. I envied him that. He didn't care what anyone thought of him. He wanted his parents and they were gone. It hurt, and he showed that it hurt. He was so much braver than I was. Lord, how I wished I could join him. I wanted to cry and scream, and shout that this wasn't fair, but I was now the head of our small, dwindling family; I had to stay in control, stoic, and collected. I was in charge of raising Hans now, and I stood here not even knowing how to comfort him.

Suddenly, I was pulled into a bear hug by a large woman cloaked in Shalimar and fur, "Oh, Dietrich, they were such good people. So good." She sobbed on my shoulder as I offered the comfort to her as best as I could, mechanically and awkward.

In reality, all I wanted to do was run. Run away from this reality, have a cosmic do-over. I wanted everything to be as it was before. I wanted my parents.

Chapter 27
Kaifeck

Vika had just finished feeding the chickens and collecting the eggs for breakfast, when she headed back out to collect the milk from the cows. It would soon be time to wash up and help Momma clean up after breakfast, grab a bite for herself, and then wake the kids. Zenzi would help with the morning rituals of cleaning and dressing, and walk Celie into town for school, while Vika minded baby Joey.

She really needed to get away today. In light of all that was going on, she needed a reprieve.

Vika took extra care in getting ready for practice this morning. Not a hair out of place, her best dress – the blue one with satin trim – it brought out the color in her eyes and brightened her skin. Perhaps it was the crisp air that kissed her as she walked the three miles into town that brought the rosy blush to her cheeks, or maybe the sense of freedom and singularity. For the next few hours, she was not anybody's mother or daughter. She was not required to do anything, but smile and sing. Yea, she could handle that. And if she had a few minutes alone with HIM, all the better. She grinned in spite of herself. In fact, they had been finding many moments together lately.

Damn, he was so handsome: his dark, curly hair that fell over his left eye when he laughed, his lopsided smile, one side of his mouth always reaching farther than the other. And, of course, the most alluring feature of all, the way his intense, soulful eyes looked into her when he was listening to her speak. It was almost spiritual. Nobody, seriously, nobody ever looked at her, or listened to her, for that matter, with that kind of sincerity, as if she mattered, really mattered.

There were the babies, of course. They loved her as their momma. They needed her for everything. This was different. This was another fully adult human, who needed her for nothing, yet wanted her with everything (or so it seemed). Had being a widow and a mother for the last eight years just made her delusional and desperate? Maybe a bit, however, she could not be so delusional that she misread every signal Dietrich was sending. There was a spark, no doubt about it. She would just have to wait and see where it went from here, and in the meantime, she would just try to enjoy it.

Chapter 28

She was something else. Her clumsy attempts at pretense masked a genuinely gracious heart. Dietrich had started to notice little changes in his routine that caused him to smile and worry simultaneously. He found himself taking extra time to pick out his suit each Wednesday. He also started using a new tonic from the drugstore on his hair, as well as combing it in a style *a-la Conrad Veidt*. He didn't even give these actions too much thought, that is, until he arrived outside St. Vitus. Then, he came down with all of the telltale signs of heartsickness: clammy palms, increased heart rate, and complete inability to recall how humans socialized.

Each time they talked, they connected so naturally. It was so foreign to him. This was very new to Dietrich, not that he was an unfeeling cad or anything, but he was 38 years old and had yet to find a woman who made him feel centered and flying free, both at the same time; a woman that would confirm to him that there was such thing as a soul mate. Someone that, no matter what, you continue to choose, over and over again, and even though it is your choice, you cannot help but feel the heavens cheer you on each time you do.

Truth be told, he had all but given up on the idea, becoming quite content with being alone with the occasional casual date. That was until he moved a bit south and a pretty brunette stumbled into his life and changed his plans.

Chapter 29

She stepped into the church, the warmth of the indoors and friendly faces filled her at once. She grinned and joined the gathering singers to practice up front, near the organ.

"Afternoon, Sister Gabriel," Father Traugott greeted her.

"Pastor," she nodded in reply. "Alice, Sarah," she acknowledged the other ladies, already reaching for their hymnals.

"How are you this fine day?" Dietrich smiled slightly beneath his formal greeting.

"Well, thank you," she replied, the subtle flirtation hidden under their brief exchange.

The pastor cleared his throat as he picked up his hymnal, an obvious signal that practice was beginning. "Page 53; let us begin with *From Where the Rising Sun Ascends*." Altogether, the five members of the church choir sang together, altos and sopranos in perfect concert. Vika was gifted with a strong yet delicate voice that sparkled like fine crystal in the sunlight. It was effortless and startling. She came alive here; she had confidence and purpose. Her addition to the choir, since moving in with her parents, had actually brought more members to the small church, if only for the music.

As usual, practice lasted only an hour and a half, and then the small group gathered for a light meal in the rectory. Dietrich slid casually into a chair directly next to Vika at the hearty oak table. Sarah was already talking about the soon-to-be new addition to her and her husband's household. She loved all her children so, but she had such a special bond with Sophie, she was wishing for another little girl this time. "Like your little one, Vika. Celie is beyond precious."

"She is a wonderful little girl," Vika responded.

Alice added, "She looks so much like you, dear, just beautiful. And hearing her in service last week, I do believe she shares your gift for song." Alice patted her hand that was resting on the table. She was a treasure. A widow herself, at 70, her difference was that she had a long, love-filled marriage to her childhood sweetheart, Eli. She embodied all that Vika desired to be in her old age: charm, compassion, and joy in each moment. She was a reminder that life was precious at every stage.

"And I am so glad to have her as a new addition to our first-grade class," Sarah delighted in her work. She was one of those people who were clearly made for the work they did. Vika felt equally blessed to have her as Celie's teacher.

"Celie is always so excited to share her day at school when she gets home. She just adores you."

"Well, she and my little Sophie have become fast friends. They sit right next to each other in class and play marbles together every day after lunch."

"That is so sweet," Vika responded.

"Always so well-behaved during Sunday service as well," Pastor Traugott interjected, "both of your children."

Vika smiled in response. She completely agreed, but was starting to get embarrassed over the attention. She lowered her head to focus on her fruit and cheese. Everyone went back to eating quietly, apparently hungry, for nobody even appeared to notice when Vika jumped suddenly, then smiled, as Dietrich secretly slid his hand over to her leg under the table.

Choir practice (including the meal) never lasted more than three hours. However, Vika's parents were under the impression that it was a bit longer and would not be expecting her back at the farm until four p.m.

The group went their separate ways outside of the church after lunch. Vika and Dietrich lagged behind. Each individually fumbled with gathering their things and invisible tasks, trying not to draw attention to their procrastination.

As always, Sarah walked Alice to her nearby home and settled her in for the evening, before going home to her young, growing family. Sarah was a surrogate daughter to the widow who lost her only child at a young age.

Sarah's own mother died in childbirth, so the relationship was mutually fulfilling. Alice became a part of a family filled with love and children, and Sarah became nurtured by the mother she never had.

The pastor closed himself in his office, as Vika stepped out into the late afternoon, dusky sunlight. It was crazy how simple acts of independence brought her so much joy. She spent the afternoon doing something she loved – that she was good at and appreciated for – and with people who demanded nothing of her – good people. She was slightly ashamed to admit it, but these people here were more her family than her own parents. She knew she should be more appreciative of her parents taking her back and providing a home for her and her babies, but as much as she needed it (and unmarried women had few options these days), she knew the price she paid was too high. She sighed deeply and closed her eyes, steadying herself. Her babies were safe and cared for. Any price was worth paying for that.

Lost in thought, she hadn't realized how far she had begun to walk home or that she failed to wait for Dietrich. Disappointment overcame her as she turned, considering heading back, when a hand reached around and covered her mouth from behind, dragging her off the dirt road and behind a nearby tree.

Kicking and screaming, she flailed around, hoping to make contact with something that would be damaging.

"Hey. Hey. Hey!" The deep, familiar voice chuckled as he ducked the oncoming assault. Vika stopped, her hair had fallen out of her carefully coiffed updo and her hat hung by its pins near her back. Dirt smudged her confused face as she processed the situation.

"Shit, Dietrich. You scared me to death!" Her breathing returned to normal as she playfully slapped him.

"Watch that cursing. You are a lady," he grinned at her. He was already familiar with her habit of spitting out profanities, and her struggle to stop. "My lady," he pulled her close and kissed her passionately. Their time together was restricted and intense; she was constantly aware of that. Nobody could know of their relationship. It would mean disaster for Vika. Her father was intensely obsessive about his grown daughter and had no intention to allow Vika to marry again, ever.

Chapter 30
Munich, 1909

I had resigned myself to the fact that I would never be a wealthy banker. I had left my internship at Munich Bank with reluctance. My boss accepted this but shared his disappointment, "You were on the fast track, son. This is our loss too."

"More of a loss for me, though," I grumbled. I was now Dietrich the Baker, Dietrich the stand-in parent to Hans. I had numerous new titles and no idea who I really was or how I was going to fulfill all of my new responsibilities. My future certainly looked different than it had six months ago.

Hans had been so distant since the funeral. He vacillated between sadness and anger. I never knew which one he would be, sometimes, he switched back and forth many times a day. I tried to talk with him, understand, which I did. I did understand, I just didn't know how to fix it. I was sad and angry too, and I had no idea how to stop those feelings. I think, deep down, when I tried to coax Hans into thinking everything would be okay; he knew I was full of shit. Our lives now, with me as the family patriarch, were simply turning into a constant series of trial and error.

Chapter 31
Kaifeck

Dietrich decided to pack Vika and him a picnic lunch as a surprise – with his apple strudel. They both gave separate (and equally unbelievable) excuses for not staying for the group meal after choir practice, both vowing to make sure they stayed the following week. Their relationship was a well-known and well-kept secret within their very small choir community, and what a relief that was. Vika was enormously paranoid about her family finding out about it. Judging from what Dietrich had heard around town and what she had shared about her father, he was a domineering louse. Dietrich wanted to know more, but was patient to let Vika tell him more about her, as she grew comfortable. She was worth the wait.

He had already laid out the blanket and unloaded the plates of strudel and glasses of milk on it, when Vika arrived separately at their designated spot in the woods.

"Oh my goodness; what is this?" she giggled and covered her mouth with her hands, "This is wonderful!"

He took her hand and guided her to sit on the blanket next to him.

"Okay, so what's next in the tales of Dietrich?" she laughed and snatched a piece of strudel from his plate, "Best food ever; you did not lie." Boldly, actually, Dietrich was surprised and took it as a sign she was growing more familiar and comfortable with him. She laid her head on his lap and gazed up at him as she picked off pieces of the pastry and ate them, "Please continue, Storyteller."

"Alright, but this is a two-way street. Next Wednesday, it will be 'the tales of Vika.'" Her smiled retreated for just a moment before she regained her composure.

"Of course," she said, convincing him only that the idea terrified her, "But today it is about you, and you are stalling."

He leaned back, looking up at the treetops and pieces of blue sky peeking through, "Let's see, where was I? The past two years were probably the hardest, I was running my family's bakery, watching Hans get angrier and more involved in our country's politics, and surviving the chaos of daily life with our new government." He paused and looked down at her, "Honestly, I still am not used to the Republic, but I can tell you the influence of it is much less up here than in Munich."

"I was sad to see Kaiser Ludwig go. I always liked the idea of growing up in a monarchy. It was romantic," she mused. "But all good things must come to an end; every new thing needs a period of adjustment," she quipped nonchalantly.

"True. And am I correct in assuming your family has enough resources to ride out the transition in moderate comfort?"

"What does that mean?" her tone became defensive as she sat up; alerting him that he needed to step back and diffuse this a little before they were in an all-out argument.

"All I am saying is that up here on your farmstead, you are fairly self-sustaining. Sure, you pay much, much more for supplies and receive much less at the market, but you already have so much, that it turns out okay. Am I right?"

"Well, sure, but…"

He interrupted her, "Just listen. That is not the average case for most of the German people. The streets of Munich are filled with the angry, the cold, and the hungry. This government has no idea how to regulate anything and all our money and resources are paying reparations, thanks to the signing of that stupid treaty. There is too much garbage, not enough coal, and the little bit of money most people have left is not enough to feed their families now." He too, even though poor, had started to acclimate to the mundane tranquility of Kaifeck.

"I had no idea." She looked contrite.

"I don't blame you for that. All people tend to think their reality is the only reality sometimes. It can be a challenge to see what others are going through while trying to navigate your way through your own day-to-day existence."

"How did it affect you and your brother? Is he here in Kaifeck with you now?"

Dietrich's face fell and he could feel his brow furrow. It was impossible to hide his concern for his brother, his brother who he left behind in Munich. "No, no, Hans is not with me."

Just like the other day, she was silent and didn't press, allowing him to gather his emotions and words. "Times in Munich are desperate. Everyone blames the November Criminals for Germany's plight right now and rightfully so, in my opinion, our country, and its people are dying, the war just made everything worse."

"There are groups everywhere, meeting in private, shouting from the street corner, it was just a matter of time before a young, head-strong kid like Hans would be lured in by one."

"Lured in? Were they dangerous? Wait a second," she stopped her train of thought. "Isn't he almost twenty-two now?" she asked quickly, doing the math based on what he had shared with her, "That's hardly a kid."

"True, but he was my responsibility. I guess, because of what happened with our parents, I have always seen Hans as younger than his years, needier. I always worried about taking care of him. Anyway, yes, revolution is always dangerous, Vika, and Munich is ripe with revolutionary ideas. I guess, honestly, some of these groups are just gathering and venting steam, but there were others. The others, they had some radical ideas. Yeah, I'd say those groups are dangerous."

He continued, "One day, Hans came to the bakery at 11:00 a.m. on a school day. It was after the war, and things were getting progressively more desperate in Munich. Hans had ditched school to go to one of those right-wing socialist meetings. At first, I was furious he skipped school. I had just scraped enough together to let him go back for one class at university and this was how he thanked me? The truth was there would be no more classes after this. We were out of money and he had to get a job somewhere and fast. I was all set to yell and scream at him about responsibility and his future, but before I could, he shoved this newsletter at me and started going on and on about 'making Germany great again' and 'how our people need to work hard, come together, and help one another.' It didn't sound so bad." He looked down at Vika who was rapt with her attention.

"He was on fire about this. So, I decided I would watch out for him like I always had. Instead of screaming and lecturing him about skipping classes, I decided to go to the next meeting with him and see what The German Workers Party was all about."

Chapter 32

"Your turn," Dietrich coaxed. They had decided to make the picnics a regular Wednesday thing for a few weeks while the weather was nice. They were fooling nobody with their ridiculous excuses of why both of them had to cut out before the afternoon meal with Fr. Traugott and the rest, but everyone was gracious nonetheless.

"Oh, come on, I want to hear about the meeting with Hans," she playfully whined as they walked through the forest, hand in hand.

Dietrich wouldn't budge, "No way, I want to hear about you."

"No, no, no, my story isn't nearly as interesting as yours, Dietrich, in fact, it's kind of sad." He didn't say a word in response to her.

"Fine, my father is very strict and quite a crumb. I grew up working on the farm, being friends with the animals, and reading Lena Christ novels in my room at night, just me, the cows, my dog, Barney, and Rumplhanni," Vika stopped talking.

"You think you're finished?" he queried.

"There's not much to tell."

"What about your husband?" She looked shocked, shocked and mad. "It's common knowledge that you are a widow," he backpedaled.

Vika's head fell and her pace slowed, "It's just…"

Dietrich stopped her and gently tilted her head to meet his gaze, "I want to know everything about you, Vika Gabriel, the good and the bad. I don't care what it is, as long as it helps me know you better."

Vika continued to look at him with fear in her eyes, closed them tightly, and then blurted out, "His name was Karl. He was horrible, and I am glad he's dead." She broke free and began walking again.

"Wow." It was all he could say, stunned by her unabashed candor and bravery. He caught up and wrapped his arms around her from behind, holding her tight, and kissing the top of her head. He felt her tightly tensed body relax a bit, and she continued, not wanting to start now that she had begun to let it out.

"The marriage was 'encouraged' by my parents. I never loved Karl. Hell, I never even liked him, but Mother told me it was a good match and that if I tried, I would grow to love him." She turned to face him again, her eyes pleading, "I tried, Dietrich; I really did try. I may not have wanted him, but I wanted a happy marriage. Nothing pleased him." She scoffed, "Well, nothing I did anyway. He was cold and he was cruel, and then he went off to fight in the war. I never even told him about Celie." She paused, waiting for shock or judgement; she got neither, "I tried to tell him, the night before he left. I fixed a beautiful meal, convinced myself this could turn out well, and then… He was so horrible when he finally got home, drunk and belligerent, I didn't tell him. He didn't deserve to know." Vika looked at Dietrich earnestly, "I was so relieved, God forgive me, I was so relieved when I heard he was killed. It was such a gift for me. He left me carrying the only good thing that ever came from him, a gift he never knew he gave."

They came upon the path that led to her farm. Dietrich knew better than to try and walk her further, "Thank you." He didn't know what else to say. He was overwhelmed by her honesty and his growing feelings for her. He embraced her strongly, trying to express all this without words. When he released her, she smiled at him, kissed him sweetly, and without another word, continued on the path to her farm.

Chapter 33

Damn, I think I really am falling in love with this woman. To hear her horrors of her marriage, her honest, clear rendition, and to still think she was the most amazing woman he had ever met. There was no more thinking about it; Dietrich was in love with her.

He could not wipe the smile from my face. It was all coming together. Yes, he knew the obstacle her father represented, the rumors, the lies, but Dietrich was certain he could put her father at ease about Dietrich's intentions for his daughter and ability to provide for her. He, too, knew about Lawrence, and as much as he disliked him, he seemed to be acknowledging his responsibility for his son. He might even welcome Dietrich lifting his burden from him. It was time. He was going to talk to Vika at the church next Wednesday, and then he would ask her father for her hand.

It was time to start really building a life here. Finally, Dietrich had to admit he would never return to Munich. He would never return to Hans. If he were truly honest, the little brother he cherished died that last night in Munich.

Chapter 34
Munich, 1914

It is strange how difficult something can seem until something infinitely more horrible arrives to take its place. It had been a few years and I was getting into the routine of taking care of Hans and the bakery, finding little time for anything else. I was managing with help from my aunt and uncle, and dear friends like Mr. and Mrs. Scheier who ran the shoe repair shop down the street. I still felt sorry for myself far more often than I should, then…well, then things got worse.

Germany declared war. Actually, Russia and Germany both declared war on each other. Munich was in an uproar. I trusted the Kaiser, and his words of solidarity among all political groups in Germany were comforting, but I had to admit, I was scared. Suddenly, taking care of Hans and the bakery did not seem like anything to complain about.

Chapter 35
Kaifeck

Now that she had let him know some of her, Dietrich seemed content not to press for more information about her past. Each week seemed like an eager blur to Wednesday. Time passed in a compendium of sweaty palms, secret meetings, stolen moments, and endless talks.

Each Wednesday was filled, not only with music and faith, but shared food and conversation with each other, just like childhood pals. It was foreign, the ease and comfort Vika felt with Dietrich now, the same as she did with Pastor Traugott, Sarah, and Alice. As cliché as it was, it was as if she had known him for years, not months. It just seemed, as of late, every Wednesday was not enough. Dietrich and Vika needed to see each other more often.

During one of their mid-week rendezvous' after practice, Vika came up with a perfect plan. "Our attic," she proclaimed proudly after they had once again discussed how to see each other more.

"I'm sorry, what?" Dietrich replied, confused.

"At night, we have a set of keys we hardly ever use. I'll give them to you. Sneak in and meet me in our attic. My parents sleep so soundly, and we'll get up before everyone and you can leave. It's perfect!"

"You are insane," Dietrich laughed.

"Do you have a better idea? Father will not let me out of his sight during the day," Vika challenged.

Dietrich shook his head, "I have nothing. I suppose we can try it."

Vika reached over and hugged him tightly. "I thought you would see it that way," she grinned broadly, as she reached for his hand and dropped the keys in it.

Chapter 36

"You're late." Her father didn't yell, but his unsmiling face and his stern, deep voice boomed as she entered the house, "You should have been home an hour ago."

"Sorry, Father. Practice ran long."

"I spoke to the pastor."

Her head fell as she stared at the floor, focusing on the pattern of the wood grain, "I'm sorry." She was not.

"Not half as sorry as you will be. It's that Praeter fellow, isn't it? Isn't it?" his voice rose.

"No daughter of mine is going to whore around using God as her defense." He yanked her hair back forcing her face to look into his, "Only for the church will I allow you to stay and sing. You will go one hour with a fifteen-minute leeway there and back: no dinner, no socializing, and right home. If I hear of any contact with this Praeter fellow again; no more choir." He let go of her hair and pushed her, causing her to fall onto the kitchen floor. Her mother stood with a look of concern and disapproval, yet doing nothing. Thank goodness Zenzi had scooted Celie and Joey out of the room when Vika arrived home, anticipating what would come.

Gathering her skirt and stepping to her feet, Vika found some courage and stepped to her father, a feat she had never attempted. With her chin jutted out and her face strong, she began, "Why? Huh, why, Father? What is wrong with Dietrich Praeter? He is a good man: an honest man, a God-fearing man!"

Her father spun to face her, "You have no need of any man. Look at the mess you made of your first marriage. Don't you think the whole town knew he was running around on you because you couldn't keep him at home? The shame you brought to your mother and me. Your life is this farm, this family, and your children. There is no need for another man." He brushed past her and grabbed his coat to go out to the barn.

Vika looked at her mother with all of the helplessness she felt. Her mother just looked back and then turned toward the evening dishes in the sink: a weakened, voiceless woman. It was then that she made up her mind. Whether he left her or not, Dietrich would know the whole truth. She would not bring her children into a relationship filled with fear, and she would not stay here. There had to be a way. She would not become her mother.

Chapter 37

Vika waited until she knew the children were asleep before she let herself cry. As she smothered her face into her pillow, she sobbed without ceasing. She wasn't sure if this control over expressing her emotions was a talent or a sign of how sick she had become. Her body shook as the sobs tore through her, with desperation to escape. Her cries were as much for the pain she experienced at the hands of her father, as they were anger at herself.

There were times when Vika convinced herself that life on the farm was normal. Days went by, sometimes weeks, when everyone acted accordingly: polite, respectful, no violence, no being called to the barn by her father. These were the times Vika began to think it was over, that she could forgive and move forward. Those were foolish thoughts, but foolish thoughts that she convinced herself were truths. Then, well then, she came home late from choir practice and the truth hit her in the face (literally).

Vika punched her mattress with her fist as she cried. She was so angry. Angry with her father for hurting her. Angry with her mother for ignoring it. Angry with herself for believing it was anything other than what it was.

Her sobs subsided as she turned on her back. Staring at the ceiling, she wiped her eyes. She made vows, vows as sacred as they ever were. She vowed never to lie to herself again. She vowed to find a way to get her children and herself to safety. She vowed to make a life for them far, far away from the farm.

Chapter 38
Munich, 1916

Due to our circumstances and the fact that Hans was only eighteen when the war started, we were not called for conscription until after his twentieth birthday, in March of 1916.

I baked him a small cake made from sugars and flour I had hoarded away in preparation for his birthday. The food rations had made delicacies like this almost unheard of. The two of us sat at our kitchen table as he made a wish, what it was he never told; we then enjoyed the cake, knowing that tomorrow we would be leaving for the army base.

"Are you scared?" I asked Hans as he shoved cake unceremoniously into his mouth.

"A little, I guess. I just want to win it and end it." He smiled up at me with cake in his teeth. It made him look like he had his two front teeth knocked out. I couldn't help but laugh.

He looked at me quizzically as I motioned to my mouth. He caught it, "Oh, oops." He laughed too, "What about you? You scared?"

"Only about you, I thought it was hard to keep an eye on you here in Munich. Now, I don't know how I am going to keep you safe. We aren't even really safe here anymore either. What if the French bomb us again? You were at school that day. I was terrified I had lost you."

"You've always taken care of me, Dietrich. I haven't always made it easy, but here I am, twenty years old and still kicking. I'll get through this too. So will you." Then, he did something so out of character. He stood up came over and locked me in a big hug, "I love you, Dietrich."

I held him tightly as if my life depended on it, "I love you too, baby brother."

"Oh, by the way, when we do win this war…" Hans started.

"What?"

"We are making a HUGE cake!" He held his arms out on either side as far as they would go, "I will be so glad to see an end to these rations. Damn."

The next morning, I closed up the bakery and asked Mr. Scheier to keep an eye on it for me. I took Hans and we headed out to Frauenkirche Cathedral for confession and morning Mass, before heading to the recruitment center.

Hans and I were going to war.

Chapter 39
Munich 1917, W.W.I.

Frank nudged me, "Come on, jackass, we are under fire!" I had dozed off, mouth agape, against the side of the bunker. I tasted the dirt in the back of my throat and came to my senses, immediately my training kicked in, and I was covering Frank with relentless fire. He sat back to reload; I grabbed a grenade.

"Pull!" he shouted.

I grabbed the grenade, pulled the pin, and shot up long enough to throw it as far as I could. All of us ducked down in the trench and covered our ears. The impact of the explosion reverberated through us. I noticed a marked decrease in our incoming fire. It was a successful hit.

I slid down the side of the trench. It had been two or three days since any of us had had any sleep, to speak of. Our bodies were wracked with the constant physical and mental strain of war. We were spent, completely exhausted. However, our lives depended on our awareness and response, so we soldiered on (Ha! Soldiered on, my horrible puns came with increasing frequency the more exhausted I became).

Eventually, the noise died down (died down). Frank and I finally collapsed in the safety of the trench. At this point, if there was a surprise attack, I think I would've just let them kill me.

Frank was checking out his image the best he could in the reflection of his Gerwher 98. "Check it out," he looked at me with his lopsided grin, "Makes me look tough, huh? Karla's gonna love this, sexy as hell." He had dodged a bayonet last week and was left with a jagged gash on his cheek that was forming into a thick scar.

"You're the toughest," I responded, as I closed my eyes and leaned my head against the back of the bunker.

Frank and I had connected early on in the infantry. Along with D.B. and Little Mikey, we all looked out for one another. We watched out for everyone in our platoon, but the four of us became fast family, for whatever reason, we just were.

Frank was a tough-talking jokester who seemed to make friends with everyone he met. I envied that, as I have never been outgoing. I was more of a head down, hardworking-in-solitude kind of guy. As jovial as he was, he knew how to work hard and he was a hell of a soldier.

Little Mikey was the youngest of us all; at eighteen, (and a young eighteen at that) he was the only surviving child of a very doting mother. He carried his mother's photo with him the way other soldiers carried their sweetheart's pictures. Physically, he was a small guy; one-hundred and ten pounds (generously), with a full face of acne, couple that with the mommy issues and he was a schoolyard bully's fantasy – and completely unfit for the trenches of war.

D.B. (His real name was Dagobert Brewster, but nobody had dared to call him that since grade school) was an enormous mountain of muscle and courage, lacking only a neck. He took Little Mikey under his wing ever since our first days in the barracks, before shipping out. He single-handedly sent five privates to the infirmary when they cornered Mikey one night. From then on, D.B. was a constant fixture at Little Mikey's side. Nobody had messed with him since.

D.B. was a re-enlist, when his time was up, he volunteered to return to fight for his country, and his country was certainly happy to have a soldier like D.B. He had no sweetheart at home and no family to speak of, just the military. He seemed to be the only person I knew who was actually happy about the war. It filled him with purpose; put a glint in his eyes. I saw the same glint when he palled around with Little Mikey and watched out for him. I imagined if D.B. ever decided to have a family, he would be a really good father.

I let Frank drone on, but I opened my eyes. I knew what I needed to do, and I hated it. I looked around surveying the trench. The soldiers in the platoon that were lucky enough to live another day were up and checking on the dead and wounded lying around them – and there were a lot. I got up and started to my left. I quickened my pace when I recognized a large hulking frame splayed out on his stomach. Dammit, only one person I knew was that huge. "D.B.!" I shouted, not expecting a response (which was good because I wasn't getting one). He lay on his ample chest with his arms reaching out. He had numerous bullets embedded in his back. His face immortalized, not in pain, but panic.

When I turned my head, I understood why. About ten feet outside of his reach lay Little Mikey. He appeared to be resting, as if he stretched out on his back for an afternoon nap in the field, his arms outstretched as if he were about to make a pillow out of his palms and gaze at the clouds. Only two things were missing, those white fluffy clouds and the entire left side of Little Mikey's face.

I crouched down in the bunker. Covering my face, I readied myself for what I needed to do. I stood back up and padded down my friends for their dog tags and personal effects. I made sure I grabbed Little Mikey's picture of his mom. If I made it myself, I would pay her a visit and I would share with her about the protector and friend he found in D.B., what he meant to him, what he meant to all of us.

"Holy fuck!" Frank came up behind me as I was checking D.B. and Mikey. "No, no!" He kept turning away and then turning back, as if the scene would somehow change if he did it enough times, "Son of a bitch! Come on, God, seriously?" I tuned him out. Frank continued to cuss and carry on, not sure how to deal with this loss. We'd lost men we served with before, since our first day in the field when Bruno Fischer got hit with enemy fire sticking his head out of a tank. D.B. and Mikey were family and losing them hurt. It hurt a lot. This was the first time since this bullshit war started that I was grateful Hans was not with me. Looking around, I had no idea what to do to keep him alive, or what I would do if he died in front of me. I tried not to, but my mind pictured Hans lying on the ground like Little Mikey, with his huge brain spread out over the dirt; I bent over and threw up all over my feet.

Pulling myself together, I continued down the line as I saw other soldiers doing the same from the other end of the trench. Checking the wounded (just dead for me so far), gathering personal effects, and then moving to the next poor soul. I also closed their eyes (or eye in Little Mikey's case) and said a prayer. *O My Jesus* seemed appropriate and quick, as there were many young men to visit. Frank and I met with some of the surviving members of our platoon, by now, we had deemed it safe enough to climb out of the bunker for a while and get some fresh air (well fresher); war clogs your nose with the stench of death, and I don't know if that really ever goes away.

Many of the soldiers lay on the dry grass of the field, falling immediately asleep. Even ten solid minutes of rest could be enough to keep you pushing on. Frank and I gnawed on some crusted bread and guzzled water from our canteens.

"Praeter, get up!" My sergeant kicked my boot. I looked up into the afternoon sun which was eclipsed by Sergeant Baker's hulking form, "Helicopter is landing in ten minutes; you need to be on it. Come with me."

I sat up, "What's going on?"

"Just be ready," he dismissed. "Klein, you go with him. I need to stay with the platoon."

Frank nodded, "Yes, sir."

I followed the sergeant, "With all due respect, sir, please tell me what the fuck is going on?"

Sergeant Baker sighed, moving his whole body with the weight of it, "It's your brother, Hans. It's not good. Given your, uh, special circumstances, the higher ups are allowing you to go to him. He's in a mobile infirmary about thirty minutes south of here. I'm sorry, son." He turned and walked away.

Frank put his hand on my shoulder, "Fuck man, fuck. That's bullshit. I'm so sorry, man." If he said anything else, I missed it, as the grass of the field rushed up and slapped me into darkness.

*****

The whirring of the helicopter blades and ensuing winds brought me to. "Thank you, Jesus! Man, you had me scared. Just – thump and down you go. Damn." Frank was hovering over me and quickly, maybe a little too quickly, helped me to my feet, "Come on, buddy, our ride's here. We gotta go."

We climbed in and headed out to the infirmary where my kid brother lay, probably dying, if not already dead. Frank's words from earlier that day kept running through my head. *Come on, God, seriously?*

Frank sat in silence next to me, absorbed in looking at the completely worn picture of his wife, Karla, that he kept with him. Even with its creases, you could see she was a looker. Blonde curls and pronounced dimples emerged with a coy smile. Frank softly rubbed his thumb against the face in the picture as if he could feel her alabaster skin through the paper. They had been married less than three months and he mooned over her with all the drama of a hormonal teenager.

"Yeah," Frank said to himself, touching the side of his face, "She'll think it's tough." He looked at me and grinned. I laughed in spite of myself. It didn't last long, though.

The pilot called back, "We're here, get ready to touch down."

Back to reality.

*****

The infirmary was a barrage of canvas tents of varying sizes and portable machines. Trucks came and went at lightning speed bringing in the wounded, some howling in pain, scarier still, some completely silent. I hoped Hans was howling.

We were led toward the largest of the canvas tents in the center of it all. I noticed a tent to the left of me where covered stretchers went in, and came back out empty. Before they left, dog tags were given and names recorded by a private who manned a station at the entrance: "Bruno Schultz, Karl Gabriel, Thomas Baker…"

They're storing the dead. I wasn't sure what was more gruesome: having to leave a soldier where he fell or carrying him to be stacked in the corpse tent.

"This way, Private Praeter," a nurse led me inside where there were neat, orderly rows of wounded in varying states. "Your brother is over here," she added gently.

"What happened to him?" I asked.

"He's lost part of his right foot and has taken three bullets to the torso. We have removed the bullets. Our concerns right now are the risk of infection and the possibility of internal bleeding. The next forty-eight hours will be critical." She paused, apologetically, "Given our resources here, we have done everything we can for him."

"Fly him somewhere else then. Can't he be taken to a real hospital?" I was frustrated, scared, and took it out on a clearly overworked nurse who did not possess the answers I wanted.

"It's not quite that easy, Private. Even if we had the resources to do that for every soldier who needed it, we aren't confident he could make the trip." She stopped in front of his bed, "I'm sorry."

I looked at Hans. He appeared to be sleeping. He needed a shave – desperately, and his hair had grown too long and was matted at odd angles, created by sweat and sleep, around his head. His foot was hooked up to a pulley and his chest was bare and covered with clean gauze.

"Hey there, little brother, I leave you for five minutes and this is what you go and do?"

A smile crawled across his face even before he opened his eyes, "How else am I going to get your attention, *Baker man*?"

I moved forward to sit at his side, "You look like shit, little bro."

"Find a mirror," he laughed, "You look worse, and you smell disgusting." Our laughter subsided into silence as we fought to address the reality.

"You're going to be okay, you know. Forty-eight hours and you are out of the woods. Don't screw it up, okay?"

"I won't." He started to cough, choking a bit. It was clearly painful for him. I pretended not to notice the crimson spray that landed on his gauze when he coughed. "I'm good to go," he attempted a smile.

"Can I get you something?"

"Yeah, water. Thanks."

I poured water from the pitcher at his bedside. I lifted his head gently to help him sip. He got some and dribbled the rest down his chest, mixing with the fresh blood on his gauze, making a smeared pink stain.

"I'm gonna let you rest now, buddy. I'll be here when you wake. I'm not leaving you," I started to walk away.

"Dietrich," he called out.

"Yeah."

"I'm not leaving you either. I love you."

"You too. Now get some sleep." I sat there at his side long after he closed his eyes. How had our lives become this? It had been so long since we had anything remotely resembling normalcy that I didn't even know what that would look like anymore. Right now, it was simple: normal would be my brother being alive. If that was as close as I ever got to normal again, that would be just fine with me.

*****

Outside the tent, Frank was sitting on a crate of supplies, smoking a Lucky Strike, and staring once again at his wife's photo. He saw me walk up.

"Shit man. Since you've been in there, they've brought in twenty-five bodies." He nodded toward the corpse tent, "Twenty-five! That's messed up. I hate this fucking war." Realizing too late this was a poor choice of things to say to me at that moment, "Sorry, man. I'm an asshole. How is your brother?"

I shrugged, "We'll know more in the next couple of days. They've done all they can. If he's not bleeding internally, he'll start improving. We just wait now and see."

"Waiting sucks."

"Yes, sir, it does. Give me one of those," I held my hand out to him.

"You don't smoke?"

"I do now." Neither of us said another word. There was nothing to say except for trite meaningless chatter. We were too close for that. We had been through far too much together to lower ourselves to that level. Instead, we sat in silence, smoking, and watching the bodies of the dead and wounded be delivered until well into the night.

*****

The longest two days of my life ended with my brother walking ten feet (on crutches) down the narrow aisle in front of his hospital bed in the infirmary.

"He's making great progress," said the duty nurse, "He'll be ready to go home soon."

"Home? By himself? Our parents…he'll be alone."

"No, he won't. These just arrived for you."

I looked down at the paperwork she handed me. Discharge papers for Hans and me. We were both going home. For us, the war was over.

I looked over at Hans who was sitting on his bed, chatting up a cute blonde nurse; a smile had just crossed my lips when the entire tent shook.

I.V.'s, people, beds, they flew in all directions and the intensity of the blast threw me across the tent. The explosion reverberated in my brain. My ears rang intensely while smoke, shrapnel, and flying cots and bodies vied for my attention as they rushed past my face in quick succession. I landed near the front of the tent on my back. All my air left me, and for a few moments, I was unable to breathe or move.

A muffled voice broke through the ringing, "Incoming! Take cover!"

It finally sunk in that we were being bombed. *What kind of devil bombs a hospital?* Getting some air back into my lungs, I flopped over and began to crawl on my forearms, dragging my uncooperative body behind me. I hoped I was moving in the direction of Han's bed. I found him lying near the blonde girl; they were scraped and bloodied, but overall, they seemed okay, disoriented, but okay. I pulled a bed frame over the two of them. "Stay here!" I ordered, as I then looked around to see who needed help next. My head was beginning to clear and my legs began to tingle; I knew I needed to find Frank.

There was a chaotic sea of stumbling, bleeding people searching for help and calling for friends and co-workers. Throughout the demolished tent, there were reverberating screams of agony. I had to get outside and see what was waiting for us all there. Once I opened the tent door, I wished that I hadn't. I seemed to have come upon ground zero. Trucks were on fire and on their sides, arms and legs lying helpless without the bodies to which they were once attached.

Fifty meters in front of me was a smoldering pile of canvas, wood, and people. I ran closer to see if anyone could be pulled to safety. I didn't have to get much closer to comprehend it was a fool's errand. I turned in circles, desperate to do something, to help, and knowing in equal measure that there was no help to be had. Looking down, a familiar sight stopped my heart. In the pile of carnage, a lifeless hand protruded, holding a well-worn and oddly well-preserved picture of a beautiful blonde with dimples.

Come on, God, seriously?

Chapter 40
Kaifeck

The stairs creaked slightly beneath Dietrich's weight. He waited, but nobody in the house stirred. He was petrified. How would he, a grown man, uninvited, explain what he was doing in their house in the middle of the night? What would Andrew do to Vika if he found out? Dietrich couldn't think of that right now, it was just making each of his movements more jittery and pronounced. Focusing, he continued to move up the steps as quietly as possible, and finally entered the farmhouse attic.

Vika stood and smiled before running over to him and wrapping her arms around him tightly, as if she had expected him not to show up.

"You're here," she stated breathlessly, "I set up a place over here for us to sit." She led him by the hand to a corner just under the window. She had layered blankets and propped up pillows underneath the window. Candelabras and two large beeswax candles emitted a romantic glow. He sat; it was just as comfortable as it was inviting.

Vika was wearing a crisp white cotton nightgown laced loosely in the front. Her hair was down and curled around her face and shoulders, framing her like a priceless print. Reflected in the glow of the candlelight, she was intoxicating. All Dietrich could think of, was how lucky he would be to spend forever with her.

"The keys – no problem getting in?" she questioned him, suddenly seeming a bit self-conscious.

"Easy and soundless, although the third and fifth steps creak; I'll remember that for next time," he responded. She instantly relaxed, as if his acknowledgement of his commitment to her, to them, was realized. She leaned in and kissed him gently. Right now, with her, in that moment, forever didn't seem like nearly enough time.

Chapter 41
Munich, 1918

I was able to bring Hans home a few months before the war ended. He was walking now, with only the occasional use of a cane, and soon, he wouldn't even need that.

Coming home to the bakery, after the war ended, was more joyous than I could have ever imagined. It had been a horrific two years, but it was over and Hans and I were both alive. Maybe now, Germany would get back on her feet. Maybe Hans could even start back up at university. Our possibilities were wide open in front of us.

I was tired and completely out of my depth. So much had happened. We had survived the loss of our parents. Hell, we had survived a war! We could survive the quickly forming facts that Germany was not getting back on her feet quite yet; in fact, we were rapidly sliding headfirst into an economic depression like we had never experienced.

There was a bright light in the midst of all this sadness and chaos. Our little community on the south side of Munich was very close-knit. In addition to our aunts and uncles who lived in the area, the other storeowners and neighbors would come into the bakery often to give us their business, as well as friendly advice and a helping hand whenever needed.

"Good morning, Herr Scheier, what can I get for you today?" I smiled as the cheerful, silver-haired man slowly made his way to the counter.

"Good morning, Dietrich, my boy. I think I will go with some rugelach today."

"Special occasion?" Dietrich smiled as he reached to remove the rich flaky pastry out of the display case.

"No, just feeling like a little splurge today before I head over to the shop."

"How is the shoe business going these days?"

"You know, Dietrich, everyone needs shoes, but everything is slower. People are waiting longer and longer before they bring in their shoes for repairs. In fact, I had a young man bring in a pair for repair last week that had the sole completely worn off."

"That is so sad; a reflection of our times."

"A genuine reflection of our times; they were the only shoes he had, he took them off and asked to wait while I resoled them."

I was at a loss for words, "Can I get you anything else, Herr Scheier?"

"No, but, oh, I almost forgot. My wife made way too much pickled herring and miltz. She just couldn't stop cooking this weekend. Here, I brought some leftovers for you and Hans," Herr Scheier lifted two large covered dishes out of the large bag he had carried in.

Now, first of all, Frau Scheier was a devoted wife and mother of seven children. She never had 'extra time' for even more chores that the ones she already claimed. No, I knew this food was prepared lovingly and intentionally for us, by these wonderful people who were suffering the effects of the economy just like everyone else. But, God bless them, they still gave with a smile.

I knew better than to refuse, "Thank you so much, Herr Scheier. This all looks delicious."

He was already headed back to the door, "No worries, son. You have a good day now. Give my best to Hans." He had given so freely to us since my parents died, all throughout the war, even now.

I stood at the front counter long after he left. So many horrible things were going on. All kinds of small political sects complaining and fighting, our currency continued to decrease in value many times each day, my parents were never coming home. I had every right to be depressed and angry, I told myself. I really thought after the war ended, things would get better, but they didn't. We were still hungry and now, our marks were worthless.

Then I got the opportunity to visit with a man like Herr Scheier, whose kindness was so natural. It gave me hope. If people could find ways to give of the little they had with the genuine joy he embodied, then there was still hope for the rest of us.

Chapter 42
Kaifeck

Vika came out of her bedroom in the early morning hours. It would be a half hour before anyone else was awake. She planned to start her chores on the farm early today, knowing Zenzi would wake the children and get them breakfast. She started to the family room and her breath caught in her throat. Her mother was sitting by an already stoked and lit fire, wrapped in a shawl in her rocking chair.

"Mother?" Vika inched closer. She was never up this early and certainly left the fire building to Father.

She didn't turn; she just kept rocking slowly. Vika knelt beside her chair and glimpsed her face in the firelight. The morning was still dark and the fire was all the light they had.

Vika was used to seeing her mother with bruises. Hell, she was used to seeing herself with them too. One of the things women must deal with in this home. Yet, the tears, the tears were new. Vika's mother sat, silently crying, no sniffling, no sobbing. Just tears running down her cheeks as if they were in a race. She gazed directly into the fire with a blank expression.

As she had still not acknowledged Vika's presence, she touched her hands resting in her lap. "Mother," she spoke softly. Mother turned to look at Vika and her expression changing to one of deep sorrow. There were dark purple bruises around her left eye and down her jawline.

"I'm so sorry, Victoria," she paused and swallowed hard, "I'm so sorry, I'm so weak." She clutched her hands in her lap tightly, then got up without another word and left the room, leaving Vika to digest what had just transpired between them.

Chapter 43

Vika walked to the barn to begin pitching hay and cleaning up after the animals. She ruminated over her encounter the other day with her mother.

Mother had never apologized for anything ever, neither had Father. It was just assumed they were never at fault. It was actually one of the reasons Vika apologized often to Celie whenever she was wrong. She desperately wanted her to realize not everything was her fault that grown-ups make mistakes too, and it was okay; you must make your wrongs right and move forward. As Vika grew up, she knew none of that. It was always her fault. In fact, she said she was sorry many times after beatings, knowing she hadn't done anything to deserve it. Her apologies were always accepted with a nod; a silent acknowledgement that it was indeed she who was at fault. For most of Vika's formative years, she believed it was her fault, that if she were only better at being a daughter, she wouldn't be so much of a disappointment.

It wasn't until Celie that Vika realized how brainwashed she had been. How sick it all was. There was nothing that beautiful little girl could ever do to make Vika strike her. It was Vika's blessing from God to be her mother, and she wanted her to know that every day. Vika saw herself as the lucky one when it came to her children.

Vika always began her farm chores by taking care of her dog, Barney. She loved his mangy little face, strong and kind, so gentle with her when she was a child. Her dark hair fell into her face as she crouched down to kiss him on his face, "I love you, Barney." She had this weird feeling of gratitude this morning for just being capable of love. Despite being brought up and brought back to a home filled with hate, she could love. She did love, and that gave her hope for her children. Her deep thoughts for the morning were disturbed by approaching footsteps. Vika stood quickly.

"Victoria. I need to see you in the barn," her father put his hand on her shoulder and let it slide down her arm to her waist. She knew what was coming and felt the bile rise up in her throat.

"Father, I'm feeding Barney and then I have to go take care of the cows. Maybe it can wait a bit." A high-pitched yelp came out of Barney as her father kicked him.

"Nooooooooo. Father. NO!" She fell to her knees to comfort Barney, but he growled at her, and then returned to whimpering. He would not let her get near him. She betrayed him. It was her fault he was hit.

Father wrapped his fist up in her long hair and yanked her backward; breathing his sour Whiskey sink into her face, "Do not make me wait."

He threw her forward, onto the ground as he walked toward the barn. Vika picked herself up, looking anxiously toward the house, hoping the children did not see. She caught a glimpse of them at the breakfast table, laughing at Zenzi, playing peek-a-boo with Joey. They were oblivious to what just transpired, "Thank you, God, for that." She wiped the mud from her face and smoothed her dress as she followed slowly to the barn, "God, please don't leave me. Please," she whispered, "Don't look."

Chapter 44
Munich, 1918

"How was school?" I asked, as Hans entered, flailing himself into a seat at a corner table and tossing his books down in front of him.

"Okay, I guess," he grumbled. His self-righteous angst routine hadn't taken long to return once we came back to life in Munich. I was beginning to get concerned that this was much more than a harmless, passing phase. I came from around the counter and sat across from him, "Hey, little brother, what's really going on? You can tell me."

"Am I talking to my brother or my 'dad'?" he questioned.

I took a deep breath. *Why isn't he beyond this by now?* I questioned myself. He was not going to make this easy, "Look, I didn't desire this position. I am your brother – always. I just need to look out for you a bit more pointedly now that I am responsible for you too. You can still tell me anything."

"I'm just sick of everything. Why does what I learn at University even matter when any job I choose isn't going to make me enough money to sustain life. If I won't be able to support myself, I sure as hell can never have a family. What kind of future do I have thanks to that stupid treaty and dumbass politicians."

"Okay, I get it, Hans," I touched his hand, "I really do. It is really hard right now – for everyone. It won't last forever, though. Times change, this will too. Our country will be strong again; people will be successful again. You'll see." I was silently congratulating myself for my enlightened 'fatherly' guidance when Hans disrupted my thoughts.

"Bullshit," Hans responded.

"Okay, language," I spat out, stunned at his reaction to my wisdom, "Come on, it can't last forever."

"Why not? What if our economy never recovers? What if we all starve to death waiting for things to change?"

I had no answer to that. It was a fear that often kept me up at night. I was scared too, but I couldn't let him know that, could I?

"I've been talking to some other guys in town," Hans started, and then paused, gauging my reaction. He knew I was more than aware of the various revolutionary groups forming in the area. Those that opposed the signing of the Treaty of Versailles and thought our current republic was destroying Germany.

"A lot of these guys are bad news, Hans," I started, trying to stay calm, even though I was filled with fear over my brother's obvious admiration for this group.

"Not these guys, they made sense. They have a real plan to make Germany great again, to bring back worth to our marks, to give us a future worth looking forward to," Hans' voice was rising with intensity.

"I don't know, Hans…"

"They meet regularly to talk."

All I wanted was to keep him safe and fed to adulthood, "Maybe you shouldn't talk to these guys anymore."

"You are forcing yourself to look away! You don't see the enemy right in front of you! I knew you wouldn't understand," Hans grabbed his books and slammed out of the bakery. I just sat there. I really thought I had the conversation under control. Damn, I missed my father; he would know what to do. I sure as hell didn't.

Chapter 45
Kaifeck

Dietrich reflected; it really was such a clever idea to meet in the attic at night. Nobody ever went up there and it was easy to sneak out before the others rose for the day. Well, until winter comes, that is. Being only October, there was still a bit of time before Vika and he had to face that.

For right now, he just loved the fact that he could lie next to her, love her, and spend time with just her. It really was as perfect as she had said it would be. Dietrich was also able to see another aspect of her: no makeup, no pretenses, no worries about what other people might think, just her thoughts, ideas, and laughter. It seems odd that two grown adults had to hide to be together. If he had not been experiencing it himself, he would have started a number of judgmental thoughts with, *if it were me...* But you see, it was him, and all he knew was that he had to be with her. Their truest moments happened in that attic. He found himself coming over more and more often, sometimes days in a row. He knew the frequency might heighten the risk, but it was too tempting. He was already imagining a lifetime with this woman. If they had to play this game for the moment to have their future together, so be it. As much as Dietrich loved how she was with him, he equally loved who he was with her. He became open, light-hearted, and hopeful. His moments with her were the closest he come to ever forgiving himself.

Chapter 46
Munich, 1918

Regardless of Hans' fumbling angrily toward adulthood, I had to work. Okay, to tell the truth, I was way too easy on him. I knew he should be working also. I knew we needed the money desperately, but I always wanted to protect him, provide for him, he was forever a child to me, to both of our detriment.

I woke him. When he didn't have his class, he now spent his days at the library. I left day-old rolls from the bakery for breakfast with some water. Our milk had run out a few days ago, and we didn't have the money to buy more, not right now.

Hans got up when I woke him, but refused to speak to me, instead, he met my gaze with a defiant scowl. *I had to fix this,* I thought. I just had no idea how to do so.

I headed toward the bakery. I hoped that today would be a successful day. However, for obvious reason, we got fewer and fewer customers coming in, finding baked goods a luxury rather than a necessity these days.

The first few hours I was open, we had one customer: an elderly widow that came in once a month to buy our day-old bread at half-price. Thinking of Herr Scheier, I gave it to her at no cost. No milk today, either, I guess, but that felt really great.

I washed and rewashed the display case, half-empty due to the inability to buy ingredients like we used to. Despite all of that, there was no reason the bakery could not be clean and inviting to the few customers that still came in.

As if on cue, the bell on the front entrance jingled, and Fanny and Fritz Braun came in. I smiled. I knew I could count on them. They were as regular as the hands on a clock. Every Saturday, they came in with their three young daughters to buy a loaf of bread and a cookie for each child.

It was a sweet and reassuring ritual. Just like Herr and Frau Scheier's generosity, it was a reminder for me that there was still room for hope. This young family continued this ritual to the delight of their daughters, no matter the economic climate. I was certain the sacrifice was much harder now, but the children's cries of delight were music in the midst of all the angry cries out in the streets.

I remember watching them come in back when my father was still behind the counter and there was only one child instead of three; I greeted them with a huge smile, "What a delight to see you again, Herr and Frau Braun. In fact, I have a fresh loaf ready to come out of the oven any minute. It will just take a moment to cool for you."

Fanny spoke first, "That would be delightful, dear. Thank you. I think little Eva is still deciding." She smiled toward her six-year-old daughter, whose nose pressed up against the display case admiring the different cookies and pastries.

"Momma, I want a sugar cookie, please," she expressed resolutely. Their eldest daughter, Ilse, clearly took the role as oldest seriously. She was prim, proper, and adorably polite.

"Of course, I think little Gretl will have the same," as she nodded toward three-year-old cherub in her arms.

"Eva," her father called at her impatiently. The girl with the golden curls turned to look at her father with wide eyes, "Chocolate, Papa!" She ran toward her father, leaving a greasy nose print on the glass where she had stood.

"Coming right up," I responded to the clan. As I gathered the goodies for their family, I couldn't help but wonder if I would have that someday. Yesterday, after the situation with Hans, I never thought I would want to be a father in a million years. Nevertheless, seeing this family, delighting in their trip to the bakery, made me reconsider just a little.

Herr Braun concluded the transaction as his robust wife handed out the goodies to her children.

"Thank you, Dietrich, dear. You have a wonderful day," she called over her shoulder as they left.

"Thank you. You do the same." Sometimes the little routines in life keep you going.

Chapter 47
Kaifeck

Vika was lost in thought as she made her way back home from practice that evening. Dietrich had been the first to reawaken her dream of a happily-ever-after. He loved her awkwardness, her reality. There was no need for a false persona here. Dietrich knew her. Well, most of her, and he was all in.

Her smile faded. The true test was to let him know it all, the secrets that ripped her apart inside and kept her hidden in the shadows of life. It was a risk, the biggest she would ever take, but she had to weigh the cost versus the weight she felt inside holding it in. This feeling of having the securing of someone's love for you – just you – no pretenses, promises, or change required; to feel this most genuinely was worth just about anything if it was possible. Maybe, it was time.

Chapter 48
Munich, 1919

The meeting was in the basement of a local pub. Each time I breathed in, a mixture of smoke and body odor assaulted me. Chairs were lined in neat rows facing the far wall, where an old wooden podium sat facing the presumed audience.

Hans was not put off by any of this. He happily guided me to the front row with all the eagerness of a young child on his birthday.

I sat there waiting for the room to fill – it never did, but little by little, ten to twelve men showed up and filled in the waiting chairs sporadically.

A guy, I think I heard someone call him Feder, walked tall and purposefully to the podium as if he was about to give a royal address and not talk to out of work, drunken men in a sweaty pub basement.

He was a thin, sinewy man with a narrow face and beady eyes, with a blocked-off mustache set in the middle of his upper lip. The stern look on his face, as he surveyed the small crowd, demonstrated how seriously he was taking this gathering. I knew this was not a group of men complaining about the government over some beers before going home to take comfort in their wives.

He began to talk, droning on and on for what seemed like hours. Surprisingly to me (who kept nodding off), most of the men there were giving him their full attention, including Hans. I tried to pay attention, but I was taking in the room as well. Hans would periodically take his eyes off this guy to look at me and grin excitedly as if he was saying, "See, isn't this amazing!" I grinned back, faking it for my brother, but frankly, I just didn't see it.

I remember him talking about the destruction of big banks and how they negatively affect the working class. He talked about the financial greed that was destroying our country. I could actually see the point in some of this, but he started talking about how there were certain people we would be better off without, the ones that manifested this financial greed. I thought he was talking abstractly about the banks or the government; he wasn't.

At the end of his speech, men raised from their chairs, cheering, led by a short dark-haired man, with a similar black mustache, in the front row a few seats from me on my right. They were all so intense, and none of them more so, than my brother, Hans.

Chapter 49
Kaifeck

Most days moved by in a hurried blur of chores and moments for Vika. Bedtime came quickly, the peaceful moments with Celie before collapsing into bed.

"Hush a bye baby in the treetop…" Vika smoothed the shining blonde hair out of Celie's face, smiling down at her sleepy eyes as she fought to stay awake. Even in the dark, curled up on her mother's bed, Celie was certain she would miss some sort of fun if she gave in to her exhaustion.

"Momma?" she muttered, not even having the strength to open her eyes.

"Yes, Buttercup," Vika replied, still stroking her hair.

"I'm happy God made you my mommy. I don't want anyone el…" She drifted off to sleep before finishing her sentence. Vika stayed for a while longer just staring at her. No matter whatever fears she had to conquer, she would make sure she earned the role of her mother. Celie needed to be protected, as did Joey, and Vika was the only one to do it.

"I want you to always feel this way, Buttercup," she whispered into Celie's hair, as she covered her and tucked in her stuffed doll, Muffin, beside her.

Chapter 50

"It's been a while since I've heard about your tales in Munich. Tell me more," Vika pried, as they sat on the embankment near a small brook in the forest. "I want to know why you finally decided to come here. Why did you leave Munich?"

"I didn't, not right way. After that last meeting with my brother, I became increasingly uneasy with this group of men to which he had become so close. Some of what they said made sense, and I got that. I mean, who doesn't want to end the poverty of their nation and make their families part of something strong and noble? It was just, this wasn't strong or noble, and Hans was getting more deeply involved."

"Couldn't you reason with him? Explain what you thought?"

"Don't you think I tried? I even kept going to the meetings with him to show him how open-minded I was to his new philosophies. All that did was drive us further apart."

"How?"

"He believed it all. He was enamored with this man, the one, who was at the first meeting I went to, that led the ovation. He spoke at most of the other meetings. Hans thought he was brilliant."

"I remember the last meeting I went to, that same guy was standing at the podium. He was not an imposing figure: a short, unassuming, mustachioed man. He did have a command when he spoke, though. I will give him that. He started by talking about all those things I agreed with: working together to rebuild Germany, making the state provide an opportunity for everyone to earn a living, outlawing child labor – these things sounded great. But then…"

"Then?"

"He started talking about denying citizenship to anyone that was not German, and to all people of Jewish descent. I didn't think that made sense. Why not help all people living and working in Germany? Why didn't we all strive to work together for a strong country, like he initially said?"

"I appeared to be the only one questioning this because the more he talked, the more charged the 'now packed' room of men became. This sounds crazy, Vika, but I was a bit frightened by it all."

"Why were you afraid?"

"He was so angry. As he spoke, he shook, his face flushed, he pounded on that weak podium with his fist as he spoke, until I thought it would break. The more he explained 'the enemy,' the more engaged the crowd became."

"All I could think was how can these people, who are suffering the same economic pains we are, side by side with us, be the problem? Their shops are suffering too. Their marks are worthless too. Their families are hungry too. I just didn't get it."

"Did you leave?"

"No," Dietrich looked down, ashamed, "I should have. I should have grabbed Hans by the back of his shirt and dragged him out of there, but I didn't."

"Why? You didn't agree; they were enraged and hateful. I would have left," Vika responded succinctly.

"Maybe you would have. I thought I would have. I was scared of the men in that room, such ordinary men, but they scared me into silence. That is on me. I will regret it always. Doing nothing was the worst decision I ever made."

She was silent.

"I only saw Hans once again after that night, and that was the night I left Munich forever."

Chapter 51

"Vika, we need to talk," Lawrence began. She honestly could not think of any situation where this turn of phrase would be a positive thing. This was no exception. Vika and Lawrence took the children out for a walk around the property. Finding a shady spot under a large chestnut tree, they laid a sleeping Joey on his blanket next to them, while Celie ran around on the grassy hill.

"Vika…"

"You're getting married."

Lawrence had a sudden intake of breath, "How? Yes. Anna and I are getting married, this weekend."

"I'm happy for you, Lawrence. You're a good man. You deserve this."

He started to pick at the grass, nervously. "There is more," he began, "She is pregnant."

"That explains the rush," Vika smiled, "Still, wonderful news."

"Well. Not entirely."

"Lawrence…"

"Anna wants me to stop coming around you and Joey so much…"

"So much? We hardly ever see you for more than a few minutes at a time as it is anymore," Vika's face flushed as her defense rose.

"It is just that she wants the focus on our marriage and our child, and of course, her son."

"She has always known about Joey. She cannot expect you to just relinquish your responsibilities!" Vika was irate. Who did this woman think she was? I was ready to hear Lawrence back me on this, but instead…

"Joey's not really even mine," he looked down at the grass and started picking again, ashamed of himself, but not taking it back.

Vika was speechless, "Wha… I…not even yours? Are you serious? You are the one who came up with this idea in the first place. Joey loves you! He is a year and a half old and thinks you are his father!" She was standing over him now and screaming. He jumped up and grabbed her shoulders.

"I know. I know. Will you please be quiet?" He looked down to make sure he hadn't stirred Joey from his nap. He was still obliviously asleep.

"I deserve a life too!" His tone was intense, even as he tried to whisper.

"You have one, Lawrence, why can't it include Joey?" Lawrence looked down at the sleeping baby, the innocent in all of this. "It can, just not as much," he replied.

"Now that you have a real child," Vika turned away. That was a low blow and she knew it.

"That's not fair…"

"I know. I know it's not. But Anna thinks Joey is yours, she cannot expect you to just disown him?"

Angry and rejected, Vika began to gather her things, looking down at Lawrence. She knew the threats were empty, but she was so hurt, she just couldn't stop herself, "There are ways to make you stay true to your word!" With that, she gathered her children and left him alone under the chestnut tree.

Chapter 52
Last Night in Munich, 1918

It had been about a week since that last meeting in the pub basement. Hans had spent the last week at a friend's flat. He had hoped for a more enthusiastic response from me. He didn't get it and he was pouting.

It was after hours at the bakery and Hans had finally returned. He silently entered, grabbed a towel, and began helping me wipe everything down for the night. For the first hour after he came back, he just worked. He said nothing. Finally, I opened some whiskey I had stashed in the back and slid him a drink: a peace offering. After a few 'peace offerings,' he began to talk, reluctantly at first, but steadily afterward.

We were talking and drinking. It was nice for a while. He talked about a girl he saw walking down Main Street this week and how they talked and made eyes at each other. I should have known the conversation would eventually turn. Soon, he started talking about the revolution to come that will show those 'dirty Jews.'

I threw down my towel and stopped wiping the counters. "What is your problem with the Jewish people?" I screamed in frustration, "That stupid treaty we signed is responsible for our situation right now. It will all pass; we will all work hard and it will pass." Our father taught us kindness and hard work will always pay off.

He called me a fool, a blind fool. Those 'Jew pigs' controlled commerce and were slowly taking over. If we didn't stop them from poisoning Germany, there would be no Germany left.

I was furious. *Did he hear himself?* He was just repeating more of that bullshit from the meeting last week. I had had enough. "I'm locking up," I said, "Let's go home." I snatched the keys from the counter and we headed for the door in angry silence. *Fine,* I thought. Right now, silence was better than what we were doing. He was such a smart kid; how could he be falling for this? The next moments visit me almost every night, still to this day.

We were standing outside the bakery. I was fumbling with the lock, shaking because of our argument. When I finally locked it, I swiftly turned and started in the direction of our house without looking. I ran into and knocked over another shopkeeper on his way home.

It was Herr Scheier, who owned the shoe repair shop on the corner. I had knocked him down. I reached down my hand to help him up. I remember starting to apologize. I called him 'Herr' as I always did, for he was my elder.

It happened so quickly. That is my recollection. That is my excuse. Just as Herr Scheier reached for it with a chuckle, Hans knocked my hand out of the way with such force; he slammed me against the glass window of our bakery's storefront. Glaring at me, he raged, "Don't address him as Herr, he is no German man."

"Watch where you are going, you pig!" he spat on the elderly man. He spat on him as he kicked him in the side, keeping him from getting up.

"Hans, what the hell?" I stabilized myself and tried to pull him away. With a strength I didn't know he had, he punched me, breaking my nose, "He's a Jew; he's a trespasser in our country!" I had never witnessed this kind of rage inside my brother before. He was consumed by it; out of control.

He continued kicking the old man, standing over him, shouting horrible things, many of which I don't recall except for bits and pieces. 'Dirty Kike,' 'Greedy dog.' I didn't try and stop him again. I sat in disbelief and bled. My mind replayed the kindness and sacrifice this man had shown to us and I cried. I cried, I was outraged and sick, but I didn't stand back up. I was weak. I just stared, fixated on the foreign, glassy, hateful look in my baby brother's eyes, and the wondering cries of a tender man.

*****

Dietrich left that night. Mr. Scheier died a week later. He read it in the paper. It stated the old man died of heart failure, but Dietrich knew the truth.

He still got the Munich paper; he didn't know why. He supposed he just couldn't let go entirely.

When he woke, drenched in sweat, at night, one thing tormented him above all else. One thing he could not forgive. Not Hans' actions, but his own lack of action. He didn't stand back up. He might have saved them both, but he never stood back up.

Chapter 53
Kaifeck

"Lawrence, you bastard!" Vika swung wildly at his face as he tried to dodge her hysterical slaps while gaining control of her flailing hands.

"I HAD NO CHOICE. You lied to me. You promised me! You cannot stay in that sickness with those kids! I cannot stand by and see this anymore. It's, it's disgusting."

"So you announce it to the world and bring it to the courts? You make it sound like I want what he does to me. Do you really think that? I'm trying! I'm trying as hard as I can!" She could not help but think this was more of a result of her veiled threats the other day and less about his ethical dilemma.

Lawrence looked down and scuffed the dirt on the ground with his feet. His dark hair falling across his eyes. "I don't know anymore, Vika," he said, looking up to her with tears in his eyes. "You are such a dear, dear friend. I agreed to pretend to be Joey's father. I love that little boy…and you. I just thought you would stop him, get away from your father…get the kids away, but no, you STAYED. STAYED, Vika! Do you like it?"

Vika punched him hard and fast. He didn't even see it coming, "How. Dare. You! Want this? WANT THIS? I've never wanted him ever, but he won't let me leave!" She paused, pacing, unsure whether she would strike him again, "It's her, isn't it? She put you up to this. Now you can get rid of Joey and me in your life once and for all!"

"Vika, please," his anger turned to empathy as he rubbed his sore jaw. He saw her tears well up and come flooding out.

"Don't you get it? If he is focused on me, he won't notice…notice Celie." She broke down completely, collapsing on the road, "Just go. Fuel the rumors, take part in the sanctimonious stares and join in the horrible things that get said to me in town."

Lawrence knelt down on the ground next to her. He looked worn, defeated. Vika knew no friend should be asked to do what Lawrence had done. To fake parentage for the sake of her reputation, for Joey. He had no obligation.

"Dammit, Vika. No, I don't blame you." He grabbed her face in both of his hands and looked clearly into her eyes, "I just want him to stop." He teared up again, "I can't make him stop." She saw the depth of his heart and how this situation pained him, "I thought taking it to the courts would shame him into stopping, but that man – he has no shame."

"You are my best friend, Lawrence. I appreciate all you have done for me, for Joey and Celie. I cannot ask for more."

"You don't need to. I am Joey's father. That's all anyone needs to know." He took a deep breath, "I will recant. Come what may, people will forget, and you and I will help them believe otherwise."

Vika hugged him tightly, "Thank you."

He gently pushed her back, "Promise me one thing. Promise me you will find a way to get out. He…"

Vika nodded. She knew what he was about to say, and agreed. No matter what she did, he wouldn't ignore Celie forever. She also realized as much as she promised herself she would leave, she had yet to make a move. Something had to change, and it had to be her.

Chapter 54

The practice was beginning and Vika wasn't there yet. This wasn't like her. She always arrived an hour before practice and shared in conversation and friendship with the other members of the choir – as well as a few stolen moments with Dietrich. Where the hell was she? Dietrich started to get genuinely worried when she finally strode in, ten minutes into practice, head down, and walking quickly to her place as she opened her hymnal. Avoiding Dietrich's gaze, she immediately began in time with the others on *Of The Father's Love Begotten.*

Her voice sounded as light and harmonic as always, but there was a weight on her. He knew he must speak to her.

It was the slowest hour of his life, but he was ready, she would not leave without talking with him. She grabbed her hat and said her goodbyes to the pastor and Sarah, kissing Alice on the cheek, and whispering something in her ear prior to heading for the door.

She moved quicker than Dietrich expected and he had to run after her, catching her by the arm right outside of the church doors, "Vika, please, just one minute. What did I do?"

She turned and looked at him intently for a few seconds, and then kissed him in front of God and everyone, not caring. She pulled away quickly, the same serious, intense expression on her face, and shoved something into Dietrich's palm, forcing his fingers closed around it. With that, she turned and rushed into the woods and home.

Chapter 55

Dietrich returned quickly to the church and made hasty excuses as to why he could not stay for the afternoon meal; instead, he rushed home to his flat above the library in the center of town.

He poured himself a whiskey and sat down, finally daring to look at the sweaty, crushed paper Vika had handed him. Obviously, it was a note. His mind went wild with painful insecurities and fears he had never experienced before. Was she leaving him? What did he do? Was there someone else? Dietrich downed his whiskey in one gulp and unfolded the paper quickly, now wishing to get this over with.

My Dearest Dietrich,

My heart aches as I write this, in part because it took me so long to write, and in part because of what I must tell you. I had once hoped my father would welcome a new marriage and a new start for Celia, Joey, and I. Alas, that is not to happen. He wants me here, and for the moment, here I must stay.

I love you, Dietrich. And, if God leaves us an open window somewhere, I want us to continue together fearlessly and honestly. I have some horrible secrets. Secrets I vowed to take to my grave, but I cannot lie to you. If I am to love you wholly, I must allow you the same opportunity to love me.

I have shared with you the horrors of my first marriage, but sadly, that is not the worst of my story. I even lied to you about my dalliance with Lawrence. You were very understanding, but it wasn't true. I had never been with anyone after my husband. Not by choice.

I know we addressed the accusations and rumors about my little Joey, and you have tolerated Lawrence as his father, but he is not. Joey's parentage and my shame are now clear.

Lawrence is a good man who wanted a new start for my children and me, and took on the burden of a lie and the public shame that accompanied it, to do so. He is now and has never been a threat to you. You are now and will always be the only man I have ever loved.

My father is a monster, Dietrich, for so long, only my monster, which helped me justify staying here. However, as Celie gets older, I see the way he looks at her, and I WILL NOT LET THAT HAPPEN. I must leave soon, and I want you to go with us.

What I have just told you might have killed every feeling you had for me. I understand and will not look to you ever, with anything but kindness and gratitude, but I love you too much to force you to love a lie. You now know everything.

If you still love me, and want to spend a life with the children and me, please meet me in the attic tomorrow night at midnight. If you are not there, I will have my answer.

My heart belongs to you always, if you will have it, Vika.

Dietrich had not realized until he saw the water droplets on the paper that he was crying, and it wasn't stopping, even as he crumpled the paper and drove his fist through the parlor wall.

Chapter 56

The next night, Dietrich entered the house cautiously, as he always did, making sure all of the lights were out and the barn was dark as well. Andrew stuck to a rigid schedule, so he had little fear of being caught coming and going in the night. Still, he stuck to his careful routine of rituals before entering with the spare set of keys Vika had given him.

Slipping out of his shoes, he carried them silently as he approached the attic steps, hesitating for a moment. It was not as if he was having doubts about Vika, quite the contrary. Dietrich loved her and was intent on getting her out of this devil's house. His hesitation had him wanting to detour into Mr. Gruber's room, beat him bloody, and then take Vika and the kids away with him now.

His was a purely emotional response to the letter Vika had written him, an emotional response that may have huge consequences. No, it is better that he talk with her first; play it safe.

The dust in the attic was visible in the air, with the reflection of the moonlight through the front window. The particles were slightly illuminated like a million little pinpoints of light. Through them, he saw her, sitting small against the wall by the window. Her feet, tucked under her chin, as she held her legs protectively. She looked like a child, a frightened child.

"You came?" she looked up at Dietrich in disbelief.

"Of course I came, Vika. I love you." He walked over to her and knelt down in front of her, "Not coming to you was never an option."

She took in a deep breath suddenly, as if she had been holding it quite some time, and wrapped her arms around him, intensely and desperate, "Oh. I love you. I love you. I love you." Then, she began to cry.

He held her tightly, smoothing her hair and kissing the top of her head until she was finished. A lifetime of tears and fear had to come out now that they had breached the surface. Dietrich just wanted her to feel safe and loved as it happened.

Finally, her body stilled and her breathing stabilized. Vika looked up at him. It was as if he were seeing her naked soul. Her face was red and blotchy.

Her eyes swollen from the exertion of her tears, her skin free of any makeup, and she had never looked more beautiful to him, more real than in this moment. "You still want me?" she whispered.

"More than ever and always. Yes, I want you, Vika Gruber," he smiled down into those glistening blue eyes.

"Even…knowing all that…"

Dietrich cupped her face firmly in his hands, "You are not what that monster did to you. He does not define who you are."

She smiled. She smiled with relief and peace, and fell back into his arms. With her head rising and falling against his chest, she fell asleep.

Chapter 57

Lawrence loved married life. He always had. There are some men who are simply meant for marriage, Lawrence was one, and he just did not feel complete without a wife and family surrounding him.

Of course, in an effort to keep his new wife happy, he had also held fast to his promise to see less of baby Joey and Vika. It was hard on him and it broke his heart to imagine little Joey wondering why he so rarely came around anymore. Nonetheless, he tried to push those thoughts aside. He had done so much for Vika and Joey; he owed them nothing more. He had his own family to concern himself with now. *If I repeat these thoughts enough, perhaps I will begin to believe them*, he thought.

Lawrence was more preoccupied than ever with his new wife right now. Their beautiful baby girl, the one who hastened their trip to the altar, had died and they were absolutely heartbroken. Anna was completely inconsolable and rarely even got out of bed lately. Lawrence had to put his own grieving aside, as well as the situation with Vika, to try to help Anna heal from their loss.

Chapter 58

He loved her. There were no doubts in her mind anymore. Vika had never known this kind of security and acceptance. Her former husband never loved her, although he was fond of the money she came tied to. And her other, well experiences, could never be described as safe or gentle. Nothing had prepared her for the love she had with Dietrich. He knew everything about her: her fears, baggage, sins. He loved her kids as his own and didn't hold her past against her at all. A fresh start. He was her happily-ever-after.

Vika turned over and held Dietrich close to her one last time before leaving. She breathed deeply to savor the scent of him: a musky, dirty scent that reminded her of the strong, hardworking man he was. She kissed him on the back of her neck and pushed herself up to go. The farm would not take care of itself, and she was running late. She couldn't afford to have anyone coming to look for her. Not now. She could continue to live in both worlds for just a little bit longer, and then, very soon, she would leave the farm and all the horrible memories behind to start her new life, her new family, with Dietrich and her children. Things were finally starting to fall into place for her.

Chapter 59

Typically, the evening meal was completely uneventful. Everyone was always exhausted by the work of the day and content to eat in silent peace. Zenzi's clumsiness in serving the meal was a foreshadowing to the noise to come.

"What is wrong with you tonight, girl?" my father slammed his fist onto the table causing her to jump; she was visibly shaken.

"Sorry, sir. I haven't been myself the last few days," Zenzi looked embarrassed as she stared at the floor.

"And why is that?" he prodded, irritated.

"The noises, sir."

"Dammit child, what in God's name are you talking about? Come out and say what you mean!" his irritation rose.

"Footsteps, in the attic; I have heard them clear as the words I am saying to you. I think we have a…ghost," she mumbled at the end.

"A ghost? Dear girl, are you disturbed?" Andrew laughed at the absurdity of it all. Thank goodness he was distracted by her perceived craziness enough not to notice Vika, choking on her roast. *They cannot find out about Dietrich and me*, she thought. They had been so careful! Panic began to well up in her stomach.

"You probably imagined it, Zenzi. All farm houses creak," Vika added.

She looked at her with venom, "I did not imagine anything! I know what I heard!" Clearly, she did not fear Vika as she did Andrew.

Zenzi turned to look at Father, "I am serious. I hear the noises late at night, sometimes while I am starting the morning meal. It is not in my mind."

"Father, really, you are just encouraging her…" He put up his hand to silence Vika.

"I will take a look, and then there will be no more talk of this, and no more stumbling around at dinner. Understood?" Father got up and headed upstairs.

"Yes, sir," Zenzi replied. She then smirked at Vika, placated by Andrew's search. Mother and the children had already gone back to eating, no longer interested in the ghost stories, at least not seriously.

Celie was waving her hands by her face, "Ohhh, I'm a ghost," making Joey giggle convulsively. Mother quietly focused on her plate. She never reacted to much of anything.

Vika tried to hide the abject terror that seized her. *Please, Dietrich; please don't have left anything behind.*

Father returned moments later, yet it seemed like hours. He quietly sat down at the table and began eating again. Zenzi came into the room and stood anxiously by his chair.

After taking a few bites, he looked up at her, "As I thought, nothing at all; it's an attic with crates and boxes and a maid with a runaway imagination," he scoffed.

Zenzi ran from the room in tears, mortified. Father looked at Vika, "I suppose you will be cleaning up after dinner tonight."

Chapter 60

Vika ran up the stairs the first chance she got. How? What? She climbed up into the attic and saw…crates. Huh? Boxes and crates were stacked and labelled. There were not any blankets or pillows from the previous night. *God, I don't know how you hid this, but thank you, thank you, thank you!* As she walked further, she found out God had a bit of help. One of the crates in the back by the small dusty window gave it away. The top was slightly askew. Vika would never have noticed had she not been looking. She lifted the top easily to see the blankets and pillows that Dietrich and she had curled up in when they met, tucked on top of some old photographs and silver plates. *God bless you, Dietrich.* She sighed, replacing the top and heading back downstairs.

Chapter 61

Oh, how Vika loved Alice. She hoped beyond hope that she would have just half of her sass and boldness when she was old. Alice was so loved and so respected by everyone (except Vika's father) who knew her, so much so that Vika's father actually feared her.

As belligerent and off-putting as he was with, well, anyone else, he could never say a cross word to Alice.

It became like a game to her. Each Sunday after Mass, Vika's Father would look around and scurry with his family from the church as quickly as he could to avoid her. Alice, about half the time, would manage to stop him before he left. Today, she had enlisted Sarah's help, who had stopped to chat with my parents about an upcoming fundraiser.

"We really must be going, Widow Frist, if you'll excuse us." Vika's father grabbed her mother's arm to sidestep Sarah's diversion, just as a sturdy wooden cane parked itself in front of his retreating feet.

"Mr. Gruber, what a delight to see you, and how are you doing this fine Sunday?" Alice's face smiled up at him. Her short stature, in no way, making her seem inferior to the tall man.

Through pursed lips, he managed, "A nice day to you, Widow Huberman. We must be getting on; my wife is not feeling well."

"Oh, I am so sorry to hear that. You know, I will help you out. I'll take Vika and the children for the afternoon. Give your lovely wife plenty of quiet to rest." *Yes, point for Alice!* Vika thought.

"Not necessary, Widow Huberman, I can handle my own. Thank you."

"Nonsense, I insist. I'll have them home before sunset." Vika and the children had already started to position themselves near Alice, "You feel better, Frau Gruber. See you next Sunday." Alice all but dismissed Vika's parents. Andrew, ready to explode, offered a tight nod and yanked his wife's arm and headed for our farm.

Sarah flanked Vika on her other side and gently grabbed Joey, "Time to go play at Alice's house!" Her kids trailed behind her as she hooked her free arm in Vika's, "Tea, conversation, and happy kids – what could be better today?"

Nothing, Vika thought. *Absolutely nothing.*

*****

"Come on, kids, I'll get you a snack and take you out to the garden." Still holding Joey, who rested on her protruding belly, Sarah led all of the kids into Alice's small, cozy kitchen, Celie and Sophie bringing up the rear skipping and holding hands. Sarah winked at them, "I'll come back with tea."

Vika assisted Alice into her favorite chair by the big picture window, placed an afghan over her lap, and sat beside her on the buttoned loveseat.

"Alice, you are amazing! I am always in awe at how you make my father cower before you."

Alice chuckled, "He doesn't scare me; besides, I have to have some time with my dear girls." She reached forward and patted Vika's knee.

Sarah came back into the room with a tray of tea, "So, how are things going with the handsome Mr. Praeter?"

"What do you mean?" Vika attempted. Both of the other women laughed.

"Please, you are not the subtlest of couples," Sarah interjected.

Vika began to look a bit fearful. Sarah backtracked, "I mean around us. You guys are never anywhere else together, and we certainly wouldn't say anything."

"You're right," Vika looked relieved. "I just can't let my father find out. He'd never approve."

"Dietrich seems like such a lovely man: responsible, religious, kind," Alice broke in.

"Father would never approve of anyone. He doesn't appear to deem my happiness a worthy cause." She sipped her tea, debating her next statement, "Things are very serious, though."

Her friends' eyes widened. "How serious?" they said in unison.

"We're going away together, with the kids. Nobody will know, not until after we are gone. Well, except for you two."

Sarah sat back speechless. Alice just sat quietly, as if she wasn't hearing anything new. She had such intuition; she probably saw this coming before the young lovers did.

"It is crazy. Some days I am overwhelmed, thinking this is what my whole life has been leading me to. I will finally have a happy family for my children with the man I love. Then..." she trailed off.

"Go on, child," Alice coaxed.

"Then I look in the mirror and I remember all I've done, I remember who I am, and know this thing with Dietrich is all foolishness, and I am destined to live and die on that farm with my father."

The silence hung heavy in the air like a blanket left on the line after a storm. Alice was the first to speak.

"Eli was my true love, 'our story was written in the stars,' he told me."

Both Vika and Sarah visibly sighed at the sweetness of that statement. "Oh, no," Alice corrected us, "It doesn't mean it was easy. I left Russia for him, my family, my home, but it was always worth it. I had Eli, and he was enough." The old woman paused, overcome with emotion, "He was more than enough; he was everything."

"Why did you leave Russia, Alice? I don't think you have ever told us," Sarah inquired.

"I was born and raised in Ukraine. My family was from Yelizavetgrad and of course, was devoutly Catholic." She looked up at us, "I will always thank them for that, and they gave me the gift of my faith. We were not especially well-off financially, but we got by and my family was well-respected in town. My father worked in textiles and my mother took good care of my eight brothers and sisters and me. Then I met Eli."

"I was only 18 when we met. He was so handsome; his eyes were both dark and bright at the same time. They were hypnotizing. I was smitten instantly."

"It sounds perfect," Vika sighed, "Happily-ever-after."

"Not quite," Alice interjected. "As I said, it was not without its troubles. If you couldn't tell by his name, Eli Huberman was not Catholic; he was a proud Jewish man. This did not go over well with my family. They were angry; they refused to allow me to see him. They even started setting up weekly dates with eligible, young, Catholic men."

"What did you do?" Vika asked.

"I defied them and saw Eli anyway. I was not a defiant girl, I always did what they told me, but this was love, and I was at its mercy completely."

"What happened?" Sarah was leaning forward as far as her pregnant belly would allow, eager to hear more.

"He wanted to marry me and my parents expressly forbade it. We ran off. We found a priest in a small parish a few miles away that was willing to marry us. It was unheard of, to intermarry a Jew and a Catholic, but thank God, he did it. We vowed to raise our children in the faith, however, as you know, that was never an issue."

"How did your parents react?"

"They were furious. They refused to allow me in their home, near my brothers or sisters, or even to speak to me for five years. Eventually, small acts of kindness from Eli – he never allowed me to hate them back – won them over. He would leave small gifts on their doorstep during Christmas. See them eating in town and take care of their bill for them. No matter what looks they gave us in the streets when we passed, he always had a pleasant smile for them. He was so good. They finally saw the great man I did. They forgave us."

"So why did you leave? It sounds like everything worked out," Vika asked.

"Things took a turn after Czar Alexander II was assassinated. Rumors, false rumors, persisted that the Jewish people did it. No Jewish family was safe."

"My parents, supportive until this, insisted I leave Eli for my own safety. I, of course, refused. We were once again, no longer welcome at the house."

"The authorities did nothing to stop the horror of what took place. Jewish homes were looted, people beaten, and some even killed. Ukraine was hit first, and we fled. I fled with Eli to a small farm town in Germany." She smiled, "I don't regret it; I know I made the right decision. You see, dear, we don't choose love, love chooses us. True love is not easy, or safe; it is necessary. The two of you simply can't belong to anyone but the other."

Vika stared at her with tears in her eyes, "I don't know if I have your strength, Alice. My situation may be bad, but it is familiar. I know who I am here, whether I like it or not."

"Or maybe, you deserve better that what others have decided you are worth. Maybe love has finally shown you your value?"

Chapter 62

Vika almost felt sorry for Zenzi as she watched her over the next few weeks. There were none of her usual snide remarks or icy stares, she simply went about her housework with her head down and her mouth shut. Vika was certain Zenzi still believed with all her heart that the farm was haunted. It showed on her face, she got spooked so easily and was so incredibly jumpy now. Vika could never tell her the truth, but she did feel guilty. Especially now.

Vika had been walking down the hallway into the kitchen when Zenzi grabbed her and pulled her into her bedroom. As surprised as Vika's face must have seemed in that moment, it was nothing compared to the expression on her housemaid's face. Zenzi was frazzled, eyes wide with fear and suspicion, all pretense of competition with her young employer had vanished; the woman was absolutely terrified and desperate.

"Zenzi, what is going on with you?" Vika inquired. Zenzi's head twitched to the side, like a dog hearing their master call them.

"Did you hear that?" Both women listened in silence for a moment and then heard Andrew's heavy footsteps go past the door.

"It was just Father coming in from outside. Really, Zenzi." Trying to disregard her responsibility for the state of her maid, Vika tried to shrug it off.

"There are no such things as ghosts. Our home is perfectly safe." Vika's air was flippant, as much as she didn't want it to be; she was so terrified of what her father would do if Dietrich and she were found out. Still, the look on Zenzi's face when she said that was devastating. Zenzi looked completely deflated, hopeless. *God, I am such an ass*, Vika thought. "Here, Zenzi, sit with me," Vika led her over to the single bed against the wall and sat next to her.

"You know, when we die, we go to Purgatory and then Heaven, or to," she hesitated, "Hell. No other places. We don't get to stay here on earth." Vika hoped the rationale of faith would ease the troubled woman's mind. Instead, Zenzi shook her head.

"I don't know anymore." She pulled two items out from underneath her pillow: a recent copy of *Borderlands* by W.T. Stead and *An Authenticated History of the Bell Witch* by Martin Van Buren.

"Why on earth are you reading these?" Vika exclaimed.

"Maybe, sometimes, souls get confused, or mad. Maybe, sometimes, they stay." Zenzi's eyes pleaded with Vika just to consider this notion. If Vika did, then maybe, just maybe, Zenzi was not losing her mind.

Vika absently flipped through the Stead's quarterly. "Well, maybe they do," she acquiesced. Still searching for some words of comfort without actually telling the truth, Vika continued, "Maybe for some reason, some souls are trapped here for a while. It doesn't mean they are bad ghosts, right?" Vika was feeling excited that this train of thought might fix everything. *Good ghosts won't scare anybody. Zenzi will be fine, and I won't be found out*, Vika thought to herself. Zenzi looked even more puzzled as she stared disbelieving at Vika.

"No, not here. The evil here eats the good until it is no more."

Vika sat back, wordlessly. Not because what Zenzi said wasn't true, but because she had no argument with it. Wasn't this the very reason she was trying to get away from this place with her kids? Her father's evil permeates everything. It makes you believe it isn't real, that you are the mad one, until it consumes you whole. Zenzi was 100% correct, maybe not about the ghosts haunting the house, but something evil certainly was.

Chapter 63

The house was alighted with chaos. Andrew was arguing loudly with Zenzi. Vika's mother, as usual, complained of a headache and went to lie down – anything to disengage.

Vika sent Celie to her bedroom with Joey and a book, then walked down to Zenzi's room and stood near the doorway. Zenzi was frantically packing. Her suitcase was open on her bed and she was just pulling things out of drawers and throwing them at the case. Some made it; some fell onto the floor. Father had his back to her, only concerned with Zenzi's mania.

"You've lost your mind!" he bellowed, "Listen to yourself. Is the farm haunted? You are a grown woman for God's sake!"

She stopped abruptly and faced him. Her voice rising to a fever pitch, "I have heard the footsteps. I have heard the voices, night after night. I have not imagined them or dreamt them." She lowered her gaze, "I cannot take it anymore. I am so afraid."

Father punctuated his boiling anger with his failure to respond immediately to her statement. With complete disgust, he very deliberately spoke, leaning very close to her face, "You are delusional and you are weak!" He picked up a skirt that had fallen to the floor and threw it in her face, "Leave now and never show your face here again!"

Vika quickly hid around the corner as Father slammed out of the room. Zenzi's sobbing could be heard clearly, even through the heavy chestnut door. Zenzi left the Gruber farm that day. They would never see her again.

*****

Not much changed after Zenzi left. Due to the fact that Vika's father was such an asshole, they did not exactly have women lined up to take Zenzi's place. Vika had always helped with the farm, but now, she took over the care of the floors and washing, as well as the dusting.

One positive was that Cas had to come out of her room more often because they needed the help and Andrew insisted she completely take over the meals.

124

He spent two days in silent indignation after Zenzi left. He still stomped around and slammed things, but no talking or yelling; it was a nice reprieve.

Dietrich and Vika continued to meet in the attic at night, but not as frequently. They began to make concrete plans for their future together, whether they were realistic or not. When Vika was with him, he had a way of making her believe that anything was possible.

Lying in his arms, snuggled in blankets on the floor, Vika closed her eyes and began to picture their ideal future. She allowed the smile to fill her face before she began speaking. She kept her eyes closed, afraid of having the reality of the dusty, cramped attic destroy her dream.

He stared at her for a moment before speaking. Her contented smile, closed eyes, and the dust particles in the musty attic illuminated by the moonlight, made her look like a child savoring the year's first snow. "Tell me what you see?" he nuzzled his face near her ear and whispered.

"No more Germany," she giggled. "We are far away from Kaifeck…and Father. I never want to step foot in this town ever again." She paused and refocused, "Ireland, I think, south-eastern, farmland, maybe near the coast. Somewhere like Waterford?"

"I like this, continue." He snuggled closer, wrapping his arms securely around her.

"We have a very small farm, just a few chickens and cows, and Barney, oh, and at least a couple of horses to ride."

"Of course."

"Maybe a pig or two, Celie really likes pigs for some reason."

"Our farm is growing," he laughed.

"I guess it is, maybe a medium-sized farm?" She finally willed herself to open her eyes and look only at him, "We are so happy. The children run and play without a care in the world. I take care of the house and make the most wonderful meals."

"It sounds like Heaven, my love."

Vika laid her head on his chest and breathed him in, smiling, "It is Heaven."

Chapter 64

She could not believe she was here doing this. This was the first truly active step she had taken toward running off with Dietrich. Finally, she was taking action instead of just thinking about it. She had to convince her father to allow her to go to the market without her mother today. Thank God for Cas and her 'headaches.' It made the perfect excuse. Andrew, irritable and overworked, mumbled and waved her off. Perfect.

Vika tapped nervously on the counter as the bank teller processed her request. She was emptying her account of every penny. This was a huge request, even with her meager fortune. Vika looked up and faced the teller's curious stare as she whispered in her manager's ear. Vika smiled what she hoped was a natural, nonchalant smile. The reality was a constipated amalgamation of anxiety and teeth that would strike fear into the hearts of youngsters. *Stop. Stop smiling.* She chastised herself. Slowly, with an attempt at being casual, she willed the sides of her mouth to lower and gazed around. Nothing to see here folks, totally natural.

The manager approached her, "Madam Gruber, what is the reason for closing out your account?"

She smiled, trying not to show the annoyance with his intrusiveness. "I just want my money," she said sweetly. "Is that a problem?" Maybe if she switched the allusion of power, he would back off.

"Oh, no, no. Not at all," he replied. "I just wanted to make sure our banking establishment has served you well."

"Quite. Thank you," she quipped, nodding slightly to dismiss him back to his work of getting her money. The manager nodded back at the teller, "Annaliese, get Ms. Gruber her money," and disappeared through a doorway.

Vika let out a huge breath that she didn't even know she was holding in. *I cannot believe that worked!*

Moments later, Vika walked out of the bank with 900 marks in her hand. This was really happening. *This is real,* she thought. *I have a future that does not involve that cursed farm or my devil of a father. I can have something else.* It seemed with each step she took, she was starting to believe that she deserved better. Her smile, genuine for once, painted her face in hope, as she walked through town and back to the farm.

*****

The next day was Wednesday. With the day her father found out about Dietrich growing more distant, it was losing its power with the passing of time. Vika had convinced him that Pastor Traugott needed to meet with them early this Wednesday to prepare a special surprise for Mass on Sunday. With each new step of her escape plan falling into place, her confidence grew. She left the house, perfectly coiffed, with her life's savings tucked securely inside her coat.

Chapter 65

Confession was a regular part of Vika's religious life. She always met with Pastor Traugott at least once monthly. There was something about the safety of the sanctuary and the privacy of the dark screen between them that evoked a deep honesty. Oh, she knew Father Traugott really knew it was her, but the sanctity of the sacrament and the illusion of anonymity was a comfort nonetheless.

"Forgive me, Father, for I have sinned. It has been three weeks since my last confession."

When she finished and received absolution, she addressed him directly, "Father, I know you know it is me. I want you to know how grateful I am for all the kindness you have shown me. You embraced me in this church when others saw me as a leper."

"My child…"

"No, wait, I just want to tell you, thank you. It may have been something you would do for anyone, but it mattered more than you will ever know that you did it for me. Thank you, Father."

Vika left the confessional, tucking the money-filled envelope beneath the small seat cushion as she went. As she shut the door quietly, she heard him whisper with finality, "Goodbye, Vika."

Chapter 66

It was risky, but Dietrich had to see her. They had promised each other not to use the attic to meet again, but this couldn't be helped. He stalked through the snow to the house. Making sure no light or noise was evident inside, he pulled out the keys Vika had given him and silently let himself in.

Taking off his shoes, he pattered to Vika's bedroom. Careful not to wake the baby or Celie, Dietrich made his way to her bed. He softly closed his hand over her mouth and gently shook her. Her fearful gasp was muffled, and subsided as soon as she registered who it was. He removed his hand and pointed up. She silently followed him up to the attic.

They settled near the window to allow the moonlight to shatter the pitch on a small section of floor.

"Why are you here?" Vika pressed, irritated. "We promised…"

"I know. I know. It couldn't be helped."

Vika's forehead wrinkled and she squinted her eyes, furrowing her brow, as she subconsciously did every time she was worried or stressed, "What…"

"I overheard something while I was eating at Café Brotgarten for lunch. The teller at Gröbern Bank, Anneliese, was talking to another girl about your visit to the bank the other day. She was talking about how strange you were acting."

Vika immediately began to defend herself, "I was so completely normal! She's strange, and she has that snaggle-tooth that makes her spit a little when she talks."

"And how nervous you seemed…"

Vika opened her mouth and then closed it again, knowing this was accurate.

"And," he continued, "that you completely closed your account?" This last part was a question to Vika.

"I know we agreed to just take a little, but we can really use it, and so could the church." She let out a breath hanging her head slightly. "In the moment, it really seemed like an unnecessary precaution," she justified.

"She said she was going to mention it to your father the next time she saw him."

"Oh, God, no." She sat back on the floor, defeated.

"Oh, yes. We have to move this up. We leave by the end of the month – no exceptions."

"Okay. In the meantime, I will make an excuse to accompany Father into town when he goes."

Dietrich reached over and kissed her deeply, cupping her face in his hands. Pulling back, he confirmed, "I will meet you in the barn at midnight on the 30th."

Vika nodded, "I love you."

"I love you too." With that, he quietly led her from the attic. She returned to her room as he put his shoes back on and let himself out, locking the door behind him.

By now, the snow had stopped. However, the air was much colder than expected and instead of filling in Dietrich's footprints with dusty snow; the existing prints were crystalized holes, demonstrating his exact route from the forest to the house.

Shit. What was he going to do? He swiftly took off his outer coat and attempted to brush snow into the prints to erase them. This proved completely ineffective. Dietrich had planned to backtrack into the woods and dust over his prints as he went. *Thanks a lot, Mother Nature*; it had been a really clever plan. A really clever plan that was obviously not going to happen.

He stood stock still at the front door, feeling utterly trapped. *If only 'the ghost' could fly me home*, he thought, laughing at Zenzi's theory. Wait, there might be something to that. If the prints had to be seen, then why not make them seem mysterious? Dietrich could use his existing prints and back up into the forest, making it look like someone came to the house and never left? This could work. Granted it was a bit of a stretch, but he would never have thought his night-time trysts with Vika would be chalked up to a haunting either.

Quickly, Dietrich threw his overcoat back on and began to retrace his steps using the encrusted prints. Soon, he was out of sight and on his way back to his flat, completely unaware that the newspaper, which he purchased in town before lunch, had fallen from his inner coat pocket as he fled.

Chapter 67

Andrew woke up earlier than usual this morning. He needed to get to the post office and bring this week's eggs into town for sale. He opened the door to start out to the barn and halted immediately. He tried to comprehend what he saw. Footprints starting a couple hundred feet out at the tree line and stopping directly in front of him at his front door. At. His. Front Door.

He became red-faced and began to rage throughout his entire body. Turing immediately around, he grabbed his rifle off the wall, slamming the door as he re-entered the house.

He made quick work of searching each room, waking his family as he went, loudly stomping in and out of rooms as he checked.

"Andrew, what is going on?" his wife questioned groggily, as she came out into the hallway.

"Son-of-a-bitch! I knew I heard something last night." He pulled the ladder down from the attic and made his way up. "I'm coming for you!" he yelled.

Moments later, he came back down. By now, Vika was standing next to her mother, with Joey in her arms and Celie by her side. Andrew looked perplexed.

"Nothing."

"Darling?" Cass began.

"Nobody. No sign of anyone up there." He walked past them all without another word.

Chapter 68

"Alice, can we talk?" Vika leaned over the old woman's shoulder and whispered.

"Of course, dear, why don't you escort an elderly woman home?" she smiled. Vika hooked her arm through Alice's and headed toward the back of the church. The congregation was thinning out, and they were coming upon Vika's parents waiting outside with the children.

"Good afternoon, Herr Gruber, Frau Gruber," Alice smiled.

"And to you, Widow Huberman," Andrew replied as he reached for Vika's other arm, "If you will excuse us…"

"Actually, I am feeling very unwell all of a sudden and really need young Vika to walk me home so I don't take a tumble." Alice looked up at Andrew with sad fluttering eyes.

Just then, Sarah walked up on the conversation, "I can take you, Alice. I don't mind."

"No you can't, precious Sarah," she answered sweetly, giving her a pointed look. "You have to help Father Traugott with the readings for next week."

"Yes, I do. I forgot. I can't take you anywhere. Sorry." Hurriedly, Sarah turned and walked (well, waddled) toward the church.

Looking back at Andrew, smiling, "Sarah works so hard; I'll have Vika home in no time. Come, children. You can keep an old woman company."

"Yippee!" called out Celie, as she picked up her baby brother and set out with her mother and Alice.

"I hate that woman," Andrew muttered under his breath, as the foursome moved slowly down the road.

*****

The children ran ahead, Celie dancing and spinning while Joey toddled after her laughing. "So, what is so important? I cannot wait to hear," Alice inquired, leaning into Vika's shoulder as they walked.

"Well, I've been thinking a great deal about you and Eli lately."

"Me too. Always do," Alice smiled.

"There were so many times it would have been easier to let him go or to find someone else, but you never did."

"Nope."

"And you never regretted it?"

"Not once."

Vika stared straight ahead at her children with a look of determined confidence on her face, "I don't think I will either."

"So it looks like you have made your decision," Alice replied, as they came to her door.

"We are leaving at the end of the month. The kids won't even know until we head out. I don't want anything to go wrong. If Father found out, it would be horrible."

"Agreed, crotchety old bastard," Alice grumbled.

"Frau Alice!" Vika responded in shock. She had never heard Alice cuss; it was delightfully astonishing.

"Well, he is. And I am more than happy for you." She stopped Vika and turned to face her, "You have always been like my own. My heart will miss you with every beat, but I am so proud of you for breaking away from this hideous devil that has shamed you into compliance throughout your years. Be strong, be free, and be happy, for you," she glanced at the children, "and for them."

"Oh, Alice. I love you so much," Vika held her tightly, not wanting to let go.

"And I love you, dear one. Why don't we go inside and have one last afternoon tea together?"

"Sounds wonderful."

Chapter 69

It had been days since her father discovered the footprints and Vika's hope was that he was forgetting about it. He went on about intruders and hearing footsteps and voices at night, but (Thank God), not once did he suggest that Dietrich may have been there, or that Vika was involved. For now, their secret was still safe, but Vika believed, with all her heart, that Dietrich was right – they must leave soon.

The recent snow had excited Celie and intrigued Joey to no end. Vika bundled each of them up carefully after breakfast so they could go frolic outside. Vika giggled to herself; she loved that word, *frolic*.

The kitchen was clean and empty, as they ate breakfast alone. Mother was in bed with a headache and Vika assumed Father was already out working on the farm.

"Let's go frolic!" Celie said, finishing her eggs. Clearly, Vika used the word quite a bit.

"Fromic!" Joey shouted, swinging his chubby hands up in the air.

"Last one out is a spoiled egg," Vika called, as the kids squealed with delight and ran out of the kitchen and to the front door. She ran after them, smiling at their laughter.

Vika stopped, bumping into the back of Celie. She realized their laughter had ceased as they silently stared into the parlor. She looked up to see what had stalled them. Without looking away, she began, "Celie, take your brother outside. I will be out in a minute." Without a word, Celie grabbed Joey's chubby mittened hand and headed for the door. As soon as Vika heard the securing 'click,' she tried to process what she saw.

Andrew sat in the corner near the fireplace facing the front door; his rifle lay across his lap. His smell assaulted her. It was obvious he had not washed in days; body odor, manure, and stale tobacco filled her nostrils. He was unshaven and his bloodshot eyes bore into the door, not even noticing her presence less than 20 feet away.

"Father?" Nothing. She crept closer, "Father?" She heard the children laughing outside, and then a thud as a snowball hit the house. This jolted Father to his feet as he started waving the gun around.

"Did you hear that?" his eyes were wild. Vika stepped in front of the gun, knowing how easily a bullet could go through the wall and into one of her children. Strangely calm, she slowly tried to ease it down with the palm of her hand.

"Father, it is just the children playing outside. Nobody is here." He allowed her to lower the barrel, but his determined grip would not relinquish control of the weapon.

"She was right," he leaned in close and whispered. Vika choked back the bile rising in her throat.

"Who?"

"Zenzi. There is something here. Nothing else makes sense." His eyes were crazy as he looked at her, "The house is haunted. We are cursed."

Chapter 70

Andrew Gruber stormed into the house, slamming the door. Nothing new. Vika hardly flinched. She was the only one around at the moment. Cas had taken baby Joey out for a stroll, and Celie was outside playing. Only Vika was lucky enough to see the latest display of hostility from her father, "Stupid mutt! Why we keep him, I have no idea!"

Vika looked up, "What did Barney do?"

"Chewed up my twine, that's what Barney did. I should just take him out and put a bullet in his head!"

"You will not!" Vika stood, "Barney is my dog, has been all my life. Maybe if you let us take him out of the barn more, he wouldn't chew on your things."

Andrew pushed her back to a sitting position in her chair, "You are as stupid as that dog is, and I will do as I please!" Andrew stormed out of the room and into his bedroom, again slamming the door for emphasis.

Vika got up as soon as he shut the door. She had to check on Barney. She knew how he treated that dog. Hell, she knew how he treated humans. She quietly shut the front door behind her and then took off in a run toward the barn.

"Celie?" As she got closer, she saw Celie furiously attacking the barn lock with tears flooding her cheeks. "Celie, baby, what happened? What did he do to you?" Vika, panicked, immediately dropped to her knees next to her little girl.

Celie looked up at her mother with dirt and tears marking her face like tribal paint, "Barney. He hurt Barney and then locked him in there. I have to help him!" She collapsed in her mother's lap, "I can't get in. I can't get in!" Barney's whimpers were clear and unceasing on the other side of the wooden door.

Vika looked at the closed lock on the barn door. Father never locked the barn, this was spite, this was to hurt them, and make the dog suffer. As she reached up and turned the lock in her hand, she was startled at the scratches and gouges in the metal, "Celie? What happened to the lock?"

Celie cried harder, her entire little body wracked with sobs, "I tried to get to Barney. Grandpa will be so mad at me!" Without looking up, she held up a scraped and bloodied little fist that held a large metal nail, "It was loose in one of the boards and I pulled it out. I was trying to get in. Grandpa will be so mad at me!"

Vika quickly took the nail and tucked it into her skirt pocket, then grabbed her child's dirty face with both hands, "No, he won't, because he will never know."

Celie's eyes got wide, "You want to lie?"

What does a mother say at a moment like this? Lying is wrong; lying is a sin; lying is bad.

"Yes, I do," Vika said. "This time, I think God will be okay with it. Now go wash yourself up at the pump and I will get Barney." She ran back to the house to get the keys and returned before Celie was finished cleaning up.

Their dog was hurt, but not as badly as he could have been. When Celie returned, she entered the barn and sat near Barney, who laid his head on her lap. She and her mother stroked the animal's fur and gave him fresh water. They sat in silence, comforting the bruised and frightened dog for some time.

"Momma?" Celie asked.

"Yes, Buttercup."

"Why is Grandpa so hateful?"

"I don't know, baby. I really don't know."

"He scares me, Momma."

Vika's stomach dropped, and she held her little girl closer to her. *Not much longer, not much longer. I'm taking you from here, baby, somewhere safe and happy. Just a few more days.* "Me too, baby. Me too."

Chapter 71

"Where are they?" Father rushed at Vika as she gathered the morning eggs. Startled, she dropped the basket, broken eggs oozing from the wicker and onto her boot. "What did you do with them?" His breath stank of whiskey and plaque.

"What?"

"You know very well what, my keys. They are gone." Vika was certain she replaced his keys after opening the barn yesterday. He had to be referring to the extra set she let Dietrich take. This time of year especially, it was not uncommon to be lax about locking the barn. They were busy and both of them were in and out of the barn continuously. It made no sense to keep it locked. The house was locked from the inside in the evening and they typically walked to town. It was quite usual to not need keys, especially an extra set, for weeks at a time.

"Father, really, why would I have them?" Vika's cheek immediately stung with his response. She instinctively took a step back as he drew closer.

"Are you mocking me? Do you think I made this up?"

"No, no, I'm sorry. I just have no use for them. I didn't mean anything." Vika had to think quickly. She never anticipated her father noticing the keys missing, and she couldn't exactly get them from Dietrich now. She just assumed he would think they were misplaced if he noticed, giving her time to get them back from Dietrich and hide them somewhere, waiting to be found.

"I will help you look. I will find them. Don't worry, Father. They are here somewhere." Her father nodded, backing off slightly, disoriented. "Father?"

He looked up at her, his anger replaced with confusion. She almost felt sorry for him – almost, "Why don't I clean this up and finish the chores, then I'll start looking. Okay?"

He nodded wordlessly, shuffling off toward the barn, where she was certain a bottle waited for him.

Chapter 72

He was drunk again. This had become increasingly common lately. It was dangerous. He would drink and wander around the house with his gun, mumbling about 'being cursed.' He had even attempted a couple of times to get in touch with Zenzi, but she refused to talk with him.

Just one more day, we can do this until tomorrow, then the children and I will finally be free.

The air was tense during the evening meal, so much so that both Celie and Joey were completely silent. Celie looked only at her plates, eager for the opportunity to scoop up her baby brother and leave the table, but too scared to ask.

The only noise coming from the table came from Father. He ate loudly, irritated, slamming his glass on the table periodically to punctuate his frustration. Vika sat nearest to Andrew, his leg bouncing furiously, his every motion exaggerated to show discontentment. She waited for the volcano to blow because it would; the only question was – how soon?

She glanced at her mother, head down, like Celie. Like herself. She really had become the legacy of the woman she reviled. Here it was, three generations of abused women, cowering in silence, as their tormentor ate his dinner. How could she really blame her mother, without too, blaming herself? The truth was finally clear: she couldn't and she didn't. She was ashamed of them both.

Andrew hurled a spoonful of stew and hit her mother in the side of the face. She didn't even flinch, just wiped it with the back of her hand. The volcano had erupted.

"You bitch; you can't even make a decent stew! Why the hell do I keep you around…?" He stood abruptly, knocking over his chair and picking up his bowl and smashing it on the floor, "Good for nothing, that's what you are." He walked to the other end of the table where her mother still sat with her head down, "The pigs eat better than this." He grabbed the back of her head and pushed her face into her stew, "Eat up, you pig!"

Vika made quick eye contact with Celie and she knew what to do. The small girl grabbed her baby brother and ran to her mother's room, locking the door. As soon as Vika heard the lock click, she was up.

"Stop it! Stop it right now! Leave her alone!" she went to assist her mother, who was now sobbing and choking out pieces of stew onto a napkin.

"You think you're something, standing up to your old man, little girl?" His hand stung her cheek, but she didn't cower, "All I do for you. This is the respect I get?" He came closer, slapped her again, and then drew her near him. He brought his face to her neck and inhaled deeply. She bit back the stew coming back up in her throat. She looked back at her mother.

Cas sat there, caught her eyes and looked away. *Do something,* Vika screamed in her mind. *Why didn't you ever stop him?*

She pushed her father hard. He stumbled backward over his own feet and fell awkwardly on the floor. The disregard, the insignificance she felt from her mother turned to rage. She looked at her mother, "I'm your daughter. You were supposed to protect me!" Vika pleaded with the broken, defeated woman who did not stand. Full of adrenaline and without a plan, Vika ran out the front door.

She ran toward the tree line. *Where the hell am I going?* she thought. She was angry, defeated, and was running on pure emotion. She wasn't going anywhere, not yet at least. She just had to move, she had to do something with this inundation of feelings that was filling her and eating her from the inside. She sat on an old stump at the edge of the woods, gripping her stomach and crying out like a wounded animal caught in a snare.

Vika heard some more crashes (probably more bowls) and screaming, followed by the form of her father, bathed in the light from the house, looming in the doorway, pausing to steady himself and then making his way toward the barn. The eruption was over. He would pass out in the barn tonight and be up early, working the farm like nothing had ever happened.

Her convulsive sobs had morphed into deep heaving breaths. Still, she rocked; still, she hurt. Her eyes had been so focused in the direction of the barn that she didn't even notice someone else had left the house also, not until she heard the snapping of twigs and the rustle of leaves in front of her.

"Oh, I really don't have anything to say to you," Vika shook her head, furious.

"You hate me," Cas said to her daughter, more as a statement than a question. "Are we really that different, you and I?"

"I don't understand. What did I ever do to you? I could never stand by and let anyone, anyone treat Celie like you have allowed Father to treat me," Vika's sobs started up again. This time, not out of self-pity, but out of the realization that she subjected Celie to this horror every day, that her mother was right, they were not so different, and that was the most devastating blow of all.

Her mother came forward and knelt next to the stump, "We are women; we suffer like no other creature on earth. It is our lot, our fate."

Vika looked at her, "No, no, this isn't right, Mother. We are human beings. We matter more than just to serve the needs of cruel men. It's a lie that we should just lie down and take it. It has to be a lie, because Celie is worth so much more than that, and if she is, then maybe we are too."

"You can leave him, Mother."

Cas looked up at her daughter with a weary smile, "I am an old woman, Victoria. Maybe it could have been different once, but I have nowhere to go. This is my fate."

"It's not mine anymore, Mother, and it won't become Celie's." She had been planning her escape for months, but only now did she realize it was really going to happen. Only now did she feel Lawrence's anger toward her for staying as long as she did. Even the most horrific and unacceptable acts become acceptable if you live with them long enough. That had been her reality, until this very moment. She was worth more than this. It was a foreign feeling, really uncomfortable, but warm and nice at the same time. She was not bound to her past; she no longer had to be.

Vika stood to return inside. She needed to talk with her daughter, who was assuredly still up, curled in the middle of her mother's bed, crying and scared. This scenario had repeated itself for the very last time. The time for talking about action was over; the time for taking action had arrived.

Cas turned to her daughter, "I'm sorry for failing you. Don't do the same to her." Vika hugged her mother.

"I won't," she whispered, "I'm going to make this right," and then headed back to the house.

Chapter 73

It was mid-afternoon. The kids were playing, although Celie was not her usual happy self. The events of last night exhausted her, both emotionally and physically. She had hardly slept at all and then spent the whole day at school.

Vika was standing by the front door, when she noticed two women coming up the road toward the house. She waited there for them. She anticipated the younger of the two was their new maid. It had been too long and it brought her some comfort to know she wouldn't be leaving her mother completely alone with her father.

The women approached the doorway. "Hello," the darker-haired woman spoke. Close-up, she looked older than Vika, but carried a sense of naivety that made her seem younger. "My name is Maria. I'm your new maid. This is my sister, Franny."

"Hello. Nice to meet you both," Vika greeted them.

"I came along to keep Maria company on her trip up here. I should be going," Franny offered.

"Nonsense, please come in. I can get you a drink before you head back out. Please come in." The sturdy blonde woman nodded slightly in acceptance and followed her sister into the Gruber home.

The two sisters sat stiffly at the kitchen table as Vika prepared cold drinks for the three of them. "Quick drink, then I must return."

Vika nodded at the new hire's sister, "Of course."

Franny consumed her drink in silence and then stood, "Thank you, I must go now, so I beat the darkness back home."

With a firm nod to both her sister and Vika, she saw herself out.

Vika smiled at the new charge, "When you are finished, I will show you to your room."

"I'm ready now. I am so excited for this new opportunity. You will not regret it."

"I'm certain we won't. You seem just lovely. Come, then, to your room," Vika guided the new woman down the hallway.

"This will do quite nicely, thank you." Maria placed her personal items and case on the oak table on the left side of the room. The room was small, but comfortably furnished. A twin bed sat across from the table and a large rustic wardrobe. Maria smiled at the delicate gold cross that hung next to the window. She smiled and turned to her new mistress, "Under God's protection."

"Well, we hope you find everything comfortable. Come with me and I will introduce you to the children."

Vika and Maria found the children outside, playing with Barney. Celie had found a hidden stash of energy; children were so resilient. The dog was chasing Celie around, trying to catch Muffin, who Celie had flying behind her in an outstretched hand. Joey sat nearby shrieking with laughter.

"You can't get me!" Celie called to the dog. Barney, always gentle with the children, playfully barked in response, but still determined to get that doll.

"Celie, honey. Come here, please. Bring your brother," Vika called.

Out of breath, Celie responded, "Yes, Momma." She took her baby brother by the hand and helped him toddle to his mother. Vika scooped him up, kissing him under his chin to hear his delighted laughter.

"This is Joey. The most contented, delightful baby you will ever hope to meet. Joey, this is our new maid, Maria." The baby just stared, sizing up the new face, as Celie came forward.

"Very nice to make your acquaintance, miss," Celie curtsied. She thought it was the height of elegance and had been dying for an opportunity to use it.

"And you, Miss Celie," Maria curtsied back, much to Celie's delight.

Yes, this was going to be a wonderful fit, Vika thought with satisfaction.

Chapter 74

Vika clutched her belly as the butterflies fluttered freely. She could not contain her excitement. She and the kids had small bags packed and hidden. She had snuck them to the attic the week prior and had now stashed them in the nearby woods. Tonight, after all were in bed, they would leave. Soon, they would be free to have the life they wanted; the life they deserved – a real family.

She felt slightly guilty about leaving her mother behind. She did her best; at least, that is what she had come to tell herself. It just hadn't been good enough. Mothers protect their children, no matter what they must sacrifice to do so. That is what Vika was doing now. Her kids would not suffer as she had.

It was almost midnight. The children, as well as the rest of the house, were asleep. She walked in circles, slowly in the barn, waiting for Dietrich. Once he was here, she would go get the kids. She heard the barn door slam behind her. "Dietrich, you will wake the whole house!" She spun around to chastise him.

It wasn't Dietrich.

Chapter 75

Vika was pushed backward with such force; she lost her footing and fell onto the hay. She looked up at the face of her father. The rage was palpable. It pulsed through the bugling veins in his face and the shaking fists compressed at his side.

"Going somewhere?" he spat through clenched teeth.

"Father, I…" She tried to get up but he shoved her back down. Submissive to him, as always. As he wanted. A moment of clarity hit her. She had worked too hard, tolerated too much. It. Ends. Now. "NO!" Vika pushed herself to standing quickly and squarely looked in his small black eyes. With all her strength and her shaking heart, she started, "I am leaving and I'll never be back, you sick fuck! I am taking my children and you will never see us again. No more victims; you don't win anymore!"

He quit shaking. He. Quit. Shaking. Vika's thoughts were racing. *Was this a victory? Maybe he finally saw her as a person, not his property. He knows he has done wrong and will step aside –*

His hand reached out and wound itself up in her hair, as he lifted her in the air and threw her. Vika's body hit the side of the barn with a dull thud that did not convey the breathtaking, searing pain that riveted throughout her body on impact. She didn't even brace herself for the fall to the ground. She couldn't get any part of her body to respond to her brain. She tried to concentrate on getting a breath. *Breathe in, just a little; just one breath.* Barney barked anxiously, pulling against his rope.

"Huuunh." Finally! Air in, air out. Coughing, Vika looked around as best she could to locate the position of her father. Hearing a noise behind her, she turned toward the door. Still disoriented, she registered that her mother was standing there, staring at her father. Her mother's face was shocking, not with terror, but resignation. The family's matriarch stood still, but slowly looked down to her daughter's broken form. Now her face changed, slowly, but significantly.

Vika saw her breathing become rapid with the hurried rise and fall of her chest beneath her dress. Her eyes narrowed and returned to the stalled figure of her husband. Like a solider in the front lines, she forged forward with a noble battle cry, already aware of her fate. She launched herself at her husband, kicking and punching; pulling his hair.

"No! You will not. You will not!" She was now on top of him, having knocked him off his feet with her weight and force, "Leave her alone!"

Vika began to push herself back toward the barn door, scooting, her eyes never leaving the horror unfolding in front of her; thinking only to get to her children and run. Run and never stop.

"Fucking Sow." Vika's father brought their mattock down on top of her mother's head, and she stopped screaming immediately, collapsing like a rag doll; her first attempt to protect her daughter quickly becoming her last. He rose to his feet, punctuating each blow with his words. "I. Will. Do. As. I. Please." The last few strikes sounded as if they were coming down into soup. A sickening slurping sound resounded as he retrieved the pickaxe out of her head, kicking the body aside, "Bitch."

His eyes found Vika near the door and he marched toward her, swinging the hatchet beside him. Unable to articulate, Vika simply looked up in terror at him, shaking her head. He quickly dragged her away from the door. He lifted her almost to standing as he swung the first blow to her face. He didn't scream, he just looked into Vika's eyes as he loomed over her. Suddenly, he dropped the mattock and fell to his knees before her. Vika's gaze met him, searching for some glimpse of humanity, as the blood poured freely from her face.

She found none.

He reached toward her and swallowed her neck with his cold calloused hands.

She lay on her back in the hay, accepting her fate reluctantly. This was the only way she was getting out. She closed her eyes and said a quick prayer, asking God to receive her. Vika almost located some peace in it all when one word shot her back to reality, fueled by strength and sheer terror.

"Momma!"

Oh God, no. Celie.

Chapter 76

This isn't good. This isn't good. Dietrich moved quickly toward the farm. He was so late. Please, Vika, know I didn't forget you. It was stupid and they would laugh about it later. The most important night of his life and his watch stops.

He needed to get to her before her father did. Dietrich knew he could take him, and he would to get Vika and the kids out of there. After knowing the disgusting things he put Vika through, Dietrich almost hoped Andrew had found out, beating his ass would feel fantastic.

Chapter 77

Maria snuggled down between the sheets of her new bed. She had put little Joey down for the night hours ago. She had begun unpacking after that, but decided against finishing. *It would be there in the morning*, she thought. She was tired and excited and just lay awake in bed, reflecting on her good fortune.

The children were adorable, and she just knew she would relish helping to care for them. Vika seemed so sweet and Maria really thought, even though she was technically her servant, that they could become good friends.

Caring for the house was no problem for her either, she actually loved to clean. She loved the rich smell of fresh soap and the shine of a clean wood floor. A clean home made her happy, and she had always appreciated the righteous exhaustion that manual labor produced.

She had said her prayers already, gazing upon the cross on the wall. *I think I have found my new home*, she thought, as sleep began to overtake her.

Maria was almost asleep when a loud banging sound from down the hall brought her back to full consciousness. Was that coming from Vika's room? She listened more. It was silent. Maybe she imagined the sound. Worrying, she began to get out of bed just as her own bedroom door lobbed open. She had only seconds to register the crazed and bloodied form of Andrew Gruber standing there before he was upon her. She didn't even have time to scream.

Chapter 78

Lights were on everywhere. This definitely can't be good. Dietrich walked quickly now from the tree line. There was light coming from the barn, as well as all through the house. It was 2:10 a.m., if all had gone according to plan, Vika and the kids were waiting for him in the barn while the rest of the house slept silently. Please, God, let them be okay. He broke into a run and was at the barn in less than a minute.

The first sound Dietrich heard as he neared was a pained howl coming from the barn. He stopped and listened for a moment to consider his approach. He feared Vika was hurt inside the barn, but that sound certainly couldn't have come from her. If Andrew was in there, Dietrich would need to move quickly to overtake him. *Damn it, I should have thought ahead and brought a weapon of some kind. Anything would be helpful at this point.*

He had no choice; he had to enter now. He could at least rush in and take Andrew by surprise. Dietrich bolted into the barn, looking around to identify where Andrew was. It took him a moment to register what he saw. It wasn't real. It couldn't be real.

The air was thick with a smell reminiscent of rotted fruit and feces. Dietrich focused in on Andrew, sitting in the middle of the barn holding Vika and crying. Was she hurt? What had he done? He couldn't see her face.

Andrew didn't even notice him, even as he came closer. Dietrich was focused only on his lover now, only on his beautiful Vika. Finally, he was able to see her face. He stopped a few feet from Andrew and emptied the contents of his stomach all over his shoes.

Vika's eyes and mouth were wide open. The terror of her last moments was captured in her expression; her tongue protruded out of her mouth, heavy and purple. Her face was in varying stages of bruising, and blood crusted to her face like old paint.

Dietrich looked at Andrew, who still didn't move; for the first time, Dietrich looked around. Where the hell was everyone else? He glimpsed behind Andrew to the body of Cas, half-hidden by hay. Then, he saw something that caused the bile to rise again as he wretched repeatedly: one little black shoe attached to a white lace sock, still twitching.

Chapter 79

The scream was piercing, loud, and agonizing. Dietrich didn't even realize it was coming from him. Looking back, Dietrich didn't even remember picking up the mattock. But he knew he did.

Andrew saw him now. The coward let her drop to the ground and got up. He just let her fall from his lap with a hollow thud: his love, his girl, a hollow thud.

She wasn't this. She was that beautiful, awkward, smiling girl he first met at St. Vitus. She was the lover who planned their future in Watersford. She was the mother who faced this monster time and time again.

*****

If love were a color, it would be blue. Blue like the water in the creek that ran through the east end of town. Blue like the spring sky. Blue like her eyes: enveloping, satiating, and endless.

This was not love, although the look in his eyes as he turned to see my first blow did set my heart a flutter ever so slightly. His face exploded in time with my rage, and again. His nose disappeared with the lower half of his jaw. He fell, twitching, as if his body was not quite sure how to respond to such brutal force. Eventually, it stopped. I did not.

I was covered, covered in his filth and metallic stench. It painted the walls and bathed the floor. I would wash it off. He never could. Not living. Not dead. His depravity was embedded in his very soul, which, about this time, should be meeting a very angry maker. I wiped my face and shook the blood from my hand, as I stepped outside.

If justice were a color, it would be red.

Chapter 80

Dietrich knew he had to enter the house. He didn't want to, but he had to. More than anything in this world, he wanted to flee this hell and forget. His heart knew what Andrew had done before he entered. Dietrich already knew what he would find.

He walked in through the open front door. For a moment, just a fleeting moment, it felt as if he was sneaking in to meet his darling, Vika, in the attic. This had become such a familiar, happy trek. Now, he came for a much different reason.

Dietrich followed the blood droplets like a depraved treasure hunter. He found the girl who must have been the new maid. The poor girl obviously fought back. She had just arrived, if only she hadn't taken this job. Going to her room first was intentional; He still couldn't wrap his mind around what he knew he would find in Vika's bedroom.

Eventually, Dietrich made his way to Vika's room. He looked everywhere but the bassinet at the end of her bed. Instead, he looked to the right at Celie's brass bed, ahead to the two wooden post beds pushed together, where Vika slept. Dietrich didn't even feel like he was still in charge of propelling his body forward. He was a marionette, at the mercy of some sadistic puppeteer who was taking him on a journey through his desecrated life.

The puppeteer let go of the strings once Dietrich glanced in the bassinet. His last conscious feeling was the crack of his jawbone on the dusty wooden floor as he passed out cold next to the broken body of the little boy he planned to raise.

Chapter 81

Lawrence and Anna had just finished breakfast. She quietly kissed him and began clearing the dishes to wash. Her son, Joey, was sitting nearby, whittling a makeshift pole to use to fish later.

Things had been quiet the last few days. They had lost their infant daughter months ago, and now, Anna was pregnant again. Last night, a spring of hope welled up in Anna. She told Lawrence she had a really good feeling about this pregnancy. She wanted so much to make him happy.

He loved her strength and hope for the future. She still grieved for the child they lost, and it may be some time before she could fully embrace the actions of this newfound hope, but she was willing. She believed in the future of their family.

Although Lawrence loved them, the new pregnancy reignited the niggling of guilt that kept him company at all times. He had not seen baby Joey or Vika in months, and his visits had been sporadic before then. Along with the shame born of neglect and abandonment, he missed them very much.

Anna was a wonderful wife, and she was clearly very determined to create a perfect family. She felt they needed nothing but the family they created to complete their happy home. To an extent, she was right, Lawrence loved her dearly and his new son, Joey. He was happy, very, very happy, but just not complete.

Lawrence realized that soon, he had to talk to Anna. He must. She had to realize his obligations and attachment to baby Joey and Vika in no way countered his devotion and love to her and their new family. He could help her overcome her irrational jealously and trust his feelings for her.

He even imagined Anna and Vika becoming friends, and Joey bonding with his baby brother; teaching him to fish and work the land.

He knew he had been unforgivably selfish. It was time to try to make things right. The enormity of Vika's heart and her love for Joey would help her forgive him.

"I'm going out for a walk," Lawrence called from the door.

"Okay, darling, I love you." Lawrence walked over to the sink and wrapped his arms around her barely protruding middle.

"I love you." He smiled and kissed her, full of hope for the future. She blushed. A soft smile crossed her lips as she went back to her work, stealing a glance at her husband as he left the house.

Lawrence walked outside; he was comforted by the smoke he saw rising from the chimney of the neighboring farm. Andrew reluctantly tolerated his presence due to the situation with baby Joey, so stopping by unannounced was never an issue. Lawrence hoped, after all he had put her through, Vika would feel the same. Anna's son came out of the house, pole in hand, "Want to come fishing with me?"

"Not now, son, later. I'll meet you down at the pond later," he tousled the hair on the top of his head with a smile. "You go; have fun."

"Okay." The boy headed off in the opposite direction, as Lawrence started walking toward the Gruber's farm.

Chapter 82

Dietrich woke as the sunlight streamed through the window. The image of the rays on the top of the bassinette battled with the reality of the stale, sickly stench of death that filled the room. He willed himself to look one more time, to force his mind to accept this sickening reality, even while it fought against him, back pedaling frantically to make up a different one. Gagging, he grabbed one of Vika's skirts and covered the baby boy.

Automatically, he started doing anything that seemed normal. He began a fire and made breakfast, although he had no intention of eating. He sat at the table with the untouched food in front of him, as if pretending normalcy would make it so.

Dietrich finally forced himself to go back to the barn. Opening the door, the smell assaulted him, wounding his senses. His eyes watered as the growing heat of the day exacerbated the situation. He set down his untouched breakfast by Barney, who laid fear-filled and hesitant near the door.

Vika… Dietrich needed to see her again. He pushed the corpse of her father away and pulled the stiffened form of his love to rest gracelessly in his lap, as he sat down in the hay stained in her blood.

It was so clear she was gone. Aside from the obvious physical brokenness, there was no reflection of her spirit in her eyes. All he now held was a bloodied, brutalized body, but it was all he had left, and he couldn't let her go. Because once he stopped, Dietrich could never hold her again.

Chapter 83

Lawrence knocked on the door, expecting an answer; perhaps a toddling Joey, happy to see him, or even an angry Vika, hiding forgiveness and relief behind a scolding stare. Instead, he was greeted with nothing.

He tried the knob, which turned with ease and entered hesitantly.

"Hello?'

Evidence of a recently cooked breakfast was on the stove along with one place setting. That didn't make sense.

"Hello... Vika?"

Lawrence started through the house quickening his pace. He found nobody. Maybe the kids were ill and Vika was caring for them in her room. One of her mother's 'headaches' could have kept her from breakfast, all of this explaining the breakfast table. Lawrence relaxed slightly, coming up with a scenario that made sense to him.

He knocked on the first bedroom door, "Vika, Mrs. Gruber?" No answer. He cracked the door open far enough to see the bassinet at the end of what had to be Vika's bed. He opened the door and walked in more boldly.

"Vika, are you okay? Vika?" The beds were empty and the bassinet was covered. In the moment he did not register the oddness of this. He backed out of the room and headed back outside.

Chapter 84

Time was no longer relevant, and Dietrich had no idea how much of it passed while he held her, but a loud sound of some kind startled him out of his daze. Dietrich lay the love of his life down on some clean hay, covering her broken face as well. He had one more loved one to visit. He stood and went over to where Celie had taken her last breath, kicking Andrew's body with intent as he went.

He tenderly scooped up the frail child, thanking God silently that her face looked peaceful; a liar's mask hiding her last moments of horror, pain, and confusion, but one that was desperately needed in this moment. His heart sank even farther as Dietrich spied her tightly clenched fists grasping golden curls, her own golden curls, ripped from her own head during her agony.

"Oh, sweet, sweet baby girl," He rocked her still form. Dietrich's pain was now taking on a powerful, physical form, and he knew it would never leave his side. *God, how I wished I could kill Andrew again!* Finally, he set her down, unable to cover her face. An irrational fear that it might scare her overtook him. Looking down, he found something familiar in the hay and reached down to take it, Celie's well-loved rag doll now stained and wet. Mere moments later, the barn door slammed open with immense force.

Lawrence stood before Dietrich with rage and pain fighting for dominance in his eyes. Taking in the scene in front of him, he soon locked in on him, confused and disheveled, standing in the midst of four bodies.

"What did you do?" he screamed.

"I was too late." And finally, Dietrich wept.

Chapter 85

Lawrence's body flew toward him, slamming Dietrich to the ground. The tears were jarred by the force of Lawrence's body, and silenced by his hands on Dietrich's throat.

"It…wasn't…me." he choked out the words as Lawrence throttled his neck, trying to gasp air into his lungs when Lawrence broke to punch his face. "It…wasn't…me."

Lawrence, himself out of breath, sat back slightly, but still pinned Dietrich to the ground, "What?"

"I didn't do this." Dietrich sucked in air greedily between guttural coughs, "It wasn't me. It was Andrew."

Lawrence turned slightly, locating Andrew's body, "Okay." He was clearly thinking now. Lawrence was a master at compartmentalizing. He choked back sobs, trying to focus completely on who did this. He had the rest of his life to grieve, and he would. For right now, he had to discover a murderer.

"Okay. Andrew, huh."

"Yes."

"Did all this."

"Yes."

"Then hacked off half his face!" Lawrence yelled.

"Ye…no. No, I did do that." Lawrence let this marinade for a moment and then slid off Dietrich, allowing him to sit up.

Covering his nose and mouth, Lawrence choked, "I can't take it. Get me out of this barn and tell me what the hell happened."

Chapter 86

They left the barn together and walked to the house. Stopping outside, they each slid down the outside wall, and sat in silence for a few minutes, not looking at each other. Slowly, Dietrich told Lawrence everything. Lawrence sat stone-faced, until he explained what waited inside the house. Even Lawrence couldn't compartmentalize the loss of the boy he claimed as his son, and the guilt of rejecting him in the past months. His sobbing was animalistic, as he punched and scratched at the ground.

As his sobbing subsided, he began to vent, "I should have killed him myself a long time ago. I knew what a sick bastard he was; I should have stopped him."

"Nobody knew he was capable of this. This isn't even human," Dietrich countered.

Lawrence turned to him, "You found them at one-two this morning?"

"Yea, around two a.m."

"Why the hell are you still here?"

Immediately getting defensive, Dietrich shot back, "I don't know, what's the protocol when your loved ones are butchered?" He fell silent for a moment. There was shock, there was the absolute horror of what he had seen, but there was only one solid truth, "I just can't bring myself to leave them."

"You can't stay here. We can't stay here. People will realize something is wrong. The authorities will come."

Dietrich shrugged.

"They will see you and the bodies and think the same thing I did. You'll hang for this!"

"I don't care. What do I have to live for now?"

"Okay, enough," Lawrence checked back into problem-solving mode.

"Eventually, you will care again, and you don't want that moment to take place on the gallows." He grabbed Dietrich's arms and forced him to stand, "We need to get started, and you need to go."

Chapter 87

Lawrence walked Dietrich to the kitchen table and made some eggs and potatoes for him to eat. He needed his strength and was rapidly losing the ability to function.

"Do you have everything in order to leave town?" Lawrence began, knowing that according to their plan, by this time, Vika, the children, and Dietrich were supposed to be well on their way to a new life together.

"I rented by the week, and yes, I haven't much, but my two small suitcases which are still hidden by the edge of trees on the west side of the property, next to theirs, I have money for travel."

"Okay, good. Help me cover up any evidence of either of us being here and then go. Don't talk to anyone; don't keep in touch with anyone. Never speak of any of this."

Dietrich looked up, a bit perplexed, "Why are you helping me? We aren't friends and I don't care what they do to me. Why do you?"

Lawrence sat down next to him at the kitchen table, "We don't have time for a heartfelt exchange right now, but here is the short version. I let Vika down. I betrayed her and Joey. I know how she felt about you, and it would be yet another betrayal if I allowed you to take the fall for this. Call it atonement if you want to, but it is the very least I can do for Vika. I can take care of you for her."

The response appeased Dietrich somewhat, and caused him to invest more in what Lawrence had to say, "Okay. What do we do?"

"First, you eat. Then start retracing your steps. Any evidence that you have been in this house, or me, for that matter, needs to be erased. I need to go home and spend some time with my family. I will eat and then say I am going to the barn to work. I'll come back for a while this evening."

Dietrich nodded, and knowing his body needed it, reluctantly dug into his meal.

Chapter 88

"Look, Papa, I caught three mackerel; Mutti's making Steckerlfisch tonight!"

"Good job, Joey," Lawrence crossed the room kitchen to kiss his wife, who was dutifully preparing the fish.

"Did you get a lot finished on the farm today? You've been out there so long," Anna commented.

"Yes, a great deal, but you know a farmer's work is never finished. I think I'll go back out after dinner and work in the barn until bedtime."

"Well, okay, dear, just not too late, alright?" Anna did little to hide her disappointment.

"I promise, my love. You know I would spend every second of the day with you if I could." He gave her a squeeze that placated her and grossed out Joey.

"Yuck," Joey mumbled from the table, causing both parents to laugh aloud.

"Just wait, Joey, someday you will meet a lovely girl that you'll want to hug all day too."

"Doubt it, unless she likes to fish."

Chapter 89

Dietrich cleaned the dishes, and set them to dry and then went about looking around the house, avoiding the maid's room and Vika's as long as possible.

After a bit of searching, he found some cleaning supplies. Grabbing the mop and metal cleaning bucket from the back closet, he filled the bucket with soapy water and mopped the wooden floor that now was caked in a mixture of mud, melted snow, and blood.

He retraced his steps, leaving the bedrooms for the very last. Avoiding the bassinet, he sat on Vika's bed with the bags she had packed for herself and the children. Lawrence had brought them in before he left. Now, he had to unpack them.

To say this task was painful would be offensive, for it was so much more. Instead of helping his new children and betrothed to unpack their bags in their new home, together as a family, he was placing the items back where they started, while his family's bodies grew cold and stiff nearby. Dietrich began with the heartbreaking task of Little Joey's clothes, so tiny. Then, Miss Celie's ruffles and lace she was so fond of. He sat staring at a yellow hair ribbon for what seemed like an hour, not being able to believe this was really happening, that this was his new reality. After placing all of Vika's clothes in the dresser, he stood facing the dresses he had just hung up. Reaching around to them with both arms, Dietrich pulled them to him, burying his face in the folds of cotton and wool, inhaling deeply the scent of her that was still on them until he had saturated them with the wet of his tears.

Finally, after building up the fire, he sat momentarily to warm up before going to tend to the animals; there was no reason for them to suffer.

Chapter 90

"Dinner was delicious," Lawrence smiled at Anna. "Now, Joey, you clean off the table and then go get washed up for bed."

"Yes, sir," Joey grumbled, as he reluctantly slid off his chair.

Turning to Anna, "I will be snuggled up with you as soon as I can. Work first, though."

"I'll wait up."

"No, really, don't bother. If you want, I will wake you when I come to bed."

She smiled, "Okay, then." And with that, Lawrence headed out toward his barn, moved quickly right past it and to the Gruber's farm.

Chapter 91

Lawrence finally arrived back at the farm, finding Dietrich in the family room with Barney. "Why did you bring him in here?" he asked.

"I couldn't leave him in there with…" Dietrich quickly amended the end of his sentence, "I couldn't leave him in there. And look," He tilted Barney's face toward Lawrence, "His eye is injured. I didn't notice it before, but it looks pretty bad."

The dog growled at Lawrence, "That dog never has been a fan of mine."

He leaned in closer anyway to check out the damage to his eye, "Easy, boy, looks painful, but I'm sure he will heal."

Dietrich stood up, laying a blanket down for Barney in front of the fire. "I cleaned everything in the main rooms and retraced my steps through the house." He paused, "I covered the bodies. I just can't look at them again."

Lawrence nodded, "Have you been in the barn again, other than to get Barney?"

He shook his head.

"That's fine. I'll go."

Refocusing himself, Dietrich continued, "I gathered my suitcases that I left by the tree line and changed, but," he glanced at the pile of bloody clothes on the kitchen table, "I don't know what to do with those."

"Burn them. Add in the towels you used to clean up. Burn everything outside while I go to the barn." With that, Lawrence left.

Chapter 92

Dietrich used one of Andrew's flashlights to guide his way to the fire pit in the dark. He set up the fire and used the bloody clothes to help kindle it. Standing back, on the clear night, listening to the crackle of the flames, feeling the cold bite of the air offset by the heat from the fire, it was almost peaceful, until he came back to the reality of what he was doing there.

The sound of a car on the nearby road shook Dietrich from his reverie. Instinctively, he shone the flashlight in the direction of the noise without thinking of the attention it may bring to him, quickly lowering it and killing the light. The car passed, and he stood out by the fire until the last bit of material burned to ash.

Chapter 93

Lawrence entered the barn while Dietrich lit the fire outside. He was grateful for the freezing air of the night, as it didn't ignite the stink of death and decomposition that was rampant here. He lit the lanterns in the barn and began near the door, systematically working his way through the hay, and thank God, he had.

Wrapping his coat tightly around him, Lawrence searched through the hay near where he had tackled Dietrich earlier, finding a key ring and a button. It may have been there forever, or it may belong to Dietrich or himself. He quickly checked his shirt, as he had not yet changed. Nope, not his. He collected them anyway and continued.

Lawrence regretted volunteering for this disgusting job, but he was fearful Dietrich would miss something significant, or snap and become utterly useless. No, his only peace of mind would be doing this himself, so he knew the search was thorough.

Unfortunately, this involved the hideous acknowledgement that he would have to search on and under the bodies. He could do this. It is a task, just a task. Be methodical. That is exactly what he proceeded to do. He lifted and examined each body before placing them in a pile of hay that he already thoroughly picked. What should have been the most repulsive of acts actually had a hint of satisfaction to it. That was when he retrieved the murder weapon – which was still stuck in Andrew Gruber's face.

Chapter 94

Lawrence had come into the kitchen after his search and handed Dietrich a burlap bag of the items he found in the barn.

"We'll talk tomorrow," he stated matter-of-factly. "Stay here, out of sight, and we will finish everything tomorrow." He turned and left with the flashlight, not even bothering to close the door as he returned to his home.

Dietrich was exhausted and clearly couldn't explain his presence if someone happened by the farm before he woke up tomorrow. He could not bring himself to sleep in any of the bedrooms and certainly couldn't sleep in a chair out in the open. He knew his answer, and it was perfect.

He climbed up to the attic, removing the blankets and pillow that Vika and he always used out of the large crate in the corner. He twisted himself in the blanket and inhaled the scent. It still smelled like Vika's perfume – a rich mixture of amber and roses. He closed his eyes, imagined she was there with him and breathed her in. It was the only peace he had felt since coming here Friday night. It was a lie. Vika was gone. However, he was desperate enough to convince himself otherwise, if only for a few moments, and fell into an unencumbered sleep.

Chapter 95

Lawrence returned from Sunday Mass with his family and sat down to a large lunch. He had hoped to already be back at the Gruber's farm by now, but making sure no one suspected odd behavior and followed him there was of paramount importance.

It was nearly two p.m. once Lawrence was able to return to the house and while he was greeted by Barney, who still sat near the fire, Dietrich was nowhere to be found. He went through the house calling for him, stopping when he noticed the stairs to the attic were down. He climbed up to find Dietrich still sound asleep.

"Alright, get up." He kicked Dietrich mildly with his foot. He wished he hadn't. He watched him wake up, realizing everything all over again. He stretched with a contented smile and then opened his eyes to see Lawrence looming over him. He registered slowly all that had happened over the last few days, looking beside him in the blankets, even though he knew she wouldn't be there. The pain returned, reopened and flowed freely.

Lawrence looked away, "I'm sorry, but we have to finish up and get you out of here. I'll be downstairs."

Lawrence waited a few minutes for Dietrich to pull himself together and come to the kitchen. He had made them coffee and the men sat at the table, sipping the drinks, with the burlap sack between them.

"What did you find?" Dietrich asked.

"A button, house keys, and I took the murder weapon."

Dietrich reached in the bag, "The keys, this is the set Vika gave me. She said they hardly ever used them."

"I'll take them and replace them somewhere in the house," Lawrence began.

"Take the button with you, and think of a place to hide the mattock. Shove the empty bag in your suitcase and take that too."

"I know just the place," he answered. Returning to the attic, Dietrich gathered the blankets and hid the mattock in between the folds before returning everything to the bottom of the crate. He tucked the button into his pocket and opened his suitcase to add the now bloodstained, burlap sack. He folded it neatly and then reached into his inside jacket pocket and retrieved the one thing he refused to burn. Dietrich gently placed Muffin carefully in the case and wrapped the sack around her. He then met Lawrence out in front of the house, "What about the dog and the animals? They are going to need to be fed again."

"Go, I'll do it before I go back home." Lawrence waved him off, "You can go now, Dietrich. Go to Ireland, go where you planned, and never come back. Get away from the evil here."

Dietrich smirked slightly and shook his head, "You mean, get away from *this* evil. Evil finds us everywhere. There is no running from it." He turned and walked toward the woods with his cases. It was ironic that he was leaving, because he knew part of him would be trapped on this farm for the rest of his life.

Chapter 96

Lawrence quickly finished taking care of the animals and moved Barney out of the house. He, too, could not fathom putting the poor animal back to the barn, so he tied him up outside and made sure he had plenty of food and water. In fact, he overfed all the animals slightly; just in case it took a while before people came inquiring about the family.

Walking home, he breathed a huge sigh of relief. He would never have imagined the events that transpired over the last few days, or the part he would play in it, but the worst had to be over. At least, that is what he told himself in order to push himself through the last few days.

Chapter 97

It was a fairly average Tuesday morning. Lawrence was out in the stable with Joey, who was feeding the horses, while Lawrence pitched the hay. As calm and rational as he tended to be, the anxiety over what was still waiting to be discovered next door made him think he could genuinely lose his mind.

He had caved and planted the seed in the mind of another neighbor, Michael, that it was odd he hadn't seen any members of the Gruber family in days. Michael concurred, and added that the family had not been at Mass that past Sunday. He left it at that, already feeling awkward mentioning it. That had been yesterday. Today, Lawrence hoped beyond hope that someone's curiosity was piqued and caused them to check on the Gruber family.

"Alright, son, time for school. Get going," Lawrence called to Joey.

"Okay, I just finished feeding them. See you after school." Joey grabbed his books and headed the two miles into school. This waiting was nerve-wracking. If nobody suggested visiting the farm by suppertime tonight, Lawrence knew he would have to.

Chapter 98

Shortly after suppertime, Michael stopped by and suggested they take a look at the Gruber farm, just in case they were ill. Lawrence tried not to let the flood of relief he felt show. He calmly agreed. Another neighbor and Anna's boys joined them. Lawrence couldn't say no without drawing suspicion that he knew what they would encounter there. As they walked over to the neighboring farm, Lawrence concentrated on their breath blowing foggy mists in rhythm as they trudged on.

A group excursion, this could not have been planned better. There would be no question of his presence there. A neighbor asked him to go. They went in a group, nothing to suspect. Lawrence shoved his hands in his pockets as he moved swiftly in the cold air.

What was that? he thought. His gloved fingers felt around, finally identifying the object in his pocket. *Oh, shit. I forgot to return the keys.*

"Look over here," called Michael from the direction of the barn. "Do they usually leave their dog outside? He looks injured." Michael tried to take a closer look and was met with a ferocious growl from Barney. He jumped back, "Damn, he doesn't like strangers. Jake, come over here and see if you can get a look at his face, he looks like he's been attacked or something."

Jacob, Lawrence, and Joey quickly followed to the barn. "Maybe he was attacked by an animal? Or struck with something?" Jake kept weaving and dodging to get a good look at Barney's eye, while the dog paced and growled at the men.

The men noticed something strange, even while the dog was certain not to come too close to the men, he absolutely refused to run away from them toward the direction of the barn door, as if he was just as frightened of something in there.

"We should probably check in the barn," said Michael. Lawrence and Jacob nodded in agreement and started forward, along with Joey.

"Joey, why don't you stay back a bit?" Lawrence cautioned his boy as they neared the barn. He would be a man himself soon, but he was still technically a child, and his child at that, and he wanted to protect him.

The cold could only stave off the decay so much, and the others knew the fate of the family the moment the air hit the nostrils of the men. "Good God Almighty!" Michael stood in disbelief at the pile of bodies inside the door.

Jacob walked past him and circled the inside of the barn. "Is that…are they all…the children?" He left it as a question.

Lawrence pushed aside the board and hay that lay on top, pulled Andrew off the other bodies, and flipping him on his back, revealed the others. Joey (who had snuck in behind them) ran outside to vomit. Jacob and Michael just stood still and stared.

"Mother of Christ," Jacob made the sign of the cross, "Who could have done something like this?"

While the emotions and shock reverberated back and forth among Michael, Jacob, and Joey, Lawrence remained immune. He had been in this barn too many times over the last few days to be shocked, and it was he, of course, that piled the bodies to begin with. "We should check the house. I don't see my boy."

He moved swiftly and purposefully to the front of the house and slid the key into the lock. "I found the keys in the door," he called out as the others caught up with him. It took only moments for the bodies of Maria and baby Joey to be found. Lawrence stayed in the bedroom with the child, hovering over the bassinet. He spotted yarn, probably from that doll of Celie's next to the child. He was removing it and putting it in his pocket when Jake entered the room.

"What are you doing?" Jacob asked.

"My boy," was all he responded. "It's my boy."

"We should get Joey out of here. I don't think it is right, having him here. He's just a lad." Lawrence didn't respond.

"…and the authorities, we must get them…now," he pressed.

"I'm staying with my boy," said Lawrence with finality, never taking his eyes off the crumpled figure in the bassinet.

"Alright then, we will bring the authorities back." With that, Jacob and Michael left to return Joey to the Bauer farm and notify the police.

Chapter 99

As much as Lawrence planned for every possibility when cleaning up the scene, the one thing he did not account for was his emotional response to being face-to-face with his baby. He had dared not look until that day. He wasn't sure what pulled him to do so, other than playing the part of discovering the bodies. He clearly understood why he found Dietrich in the barn with Vika. It was the same reason he couldn't leave the side of the bassinet. Once he did, his boy would be gone forever, and that thought was intolerable.

The neighbors would talk and the authorities would question him about his odd behavior that day. Overall, Lawrence thought he pulled it off rather well. He never mentioned Dietrich, in fact, nobody ever did. Due to the secrecy of their relationship, nobody knew about it other than himself, and Vika's friends in the choir at St. Vitus, and they always remained silent and devoted to their friend's memory.

Chapter 100
Vienna

Dietrich had always been a man of his word, and true to that, he never returned to Kaifeck, and true to his heart, he never married. He relocated, but not to Ireland. That was a place filled with a very different future for him: one that would never occur. Instead, he fled south to Austria. Hopeful that maybe here he would find peace. Thus far, that hasn't happened.

It has been nearly twenty years since Dietrich first found himself on Austrian soil.

At first, he simply existed. In fact, it surprised the hell out of him that he didn't die in those early years. He was a shell of a man; sleeping in alleyways, begging for food. Dietrich simply didn't care what happened to him; to him, he was already dead. He died in the barn in Kaifeck, that night many years ago, of that he was convinced.

Yet here he was, on the streets of Vienna, living a hell he couldn't escape. There was only one effort Dietrich put forth, one innate thing he knew to do. He went to church.

It seemed so bizarre, even in hindsight, and Dietrich could not explain it any better now than he could back then. He just showed up, every Sunday at St. Michael's Cathedral. Dietrich came after Mass began and snuck into the back row: filthy, unshaven, and too ashamed to go up for Communion. This was his only momentary reprieve from his plight.

However, a man such as this does not go unnoticed. One Sunday, Dietrich was approached by two men that changed his life.

Father Michael Donnigan was an elderly priest who had been guiding souls at Saint Michael's Cathedral for well over sixty years. He walked slightly hunched over with a slow gait. Dietrich would come to see, as he got to know him better, the walk fit him, as he was never in a hurry and had limitless patience. That day they met, before Dietrich left the church after Mass, he saw Father Donnigan starting to make his way toward him. Dietrich froze. First of all, he didn't want to disrespect a priest, who (up until now, he thought) had not shunned his filthy form from this church. Secondly, Dietrich had convinced himself that he was headed toward someone else, and a hasty escape at this point would only bring attention to him. So, he stayed, glued to the spot in his pew as the priest drew nearer (ever so slowly).

His speedier counterpart was a young priest whose name Dietrich would later find out was Alexander. Alexander tried to slow his walk enough to accompany the older priest, but could not, so he was continually getting too far ahead and having to take a few steps back and start again, trying to keep in step with Father Michael. The effect was comical, as if the younger of the two was dancing some awkward cha-cha.

Later than sooner, the two men were standing at the end of Dietrich's pew. He knew they could smell him, but neither gave any indication of offense. Instead, the elderly priest lifted his head and met his eyes. Smiling, he asked, "Are you free for lunch, sir?" His were the first pair of eyes that actually saw Dietrich since coming to Vienna, and what eyes they were. They shone with clarity and a life all their own; a brilliant blue, so much like Vika's. Except, his were surrounded by folds of skin, wrinkles and age spots, as if age itself was hiding them like some precious gems.

Dietrich was transfixed, yet did not answer.

"Come; share a meal with an old man. I believe it is somewhere in the Bible that if you refuse an old priest and make him sad, you go to Hell." That startled Dietrich, which he discovered was the priest's desired effect, he turned back toward him with those smiling eyes and chuckled, before turning back to make his way to the rectory. The younger priest, Father Alexander, responded to a nod from his mentor and quickened his steps toward Dietrich. He waited for him to rise in case he needed assistance walking. Dietrich did, and Father Alexander guided his frail shoulders as he shakily stood. Dietrich was no longer the strong rugged man that made Vika's heart beat faster. He was, maybe, a hundred-and-ten pounds, tired, weak. Father Alexander guided him to a large wooden table, sturdy but plain, in the rectory. Dietrich sat with Father Michael as the younger priest brought them steaming bowls of stew and fresh crusts of bread with cheese. Dietrich was overwhelmed and starving, he ate feverishly until he was almost ill. It was not polite or appealing, but again, neither man said a word. They simply ate quietly. Afterward, they talked. Dietrich could not recall all that was said, or even how it began, but it was so necessary. He wept until he shook, however, he was yet to reveal his deepest secrets; those were for another time. Even while still carrying that load alone, Dietrich felt more relief than he had in a very long time. One does not realize, at least, he did not, how very essential simple human contact is, until it is returned after a long deprivation. With their meal eaten and his emotions spent, the men offered Dietrich a spare bed in the rectory. They let him clean up and even gave him a set of clothes.

These two priests not only fed Dietrich that day, they took him under their wings, and nursed him back to health. Eventually, they even assisted Dietrich in going to seminary. Looking back, Dietrich had had more than his fair share of second chances. He had seen such evil, such horrendous, despicable devilry, but he had also been on the receiving end of true kindness and love from some of God's most beautiful creatures. Dietrich still didn't know if it would have ever been possible to identify this beauty without knowing torment in such vivid detail.

Father Michael died at the age of 94 in 1931. Father Alexander took over at St. Michael's until his premature death of rheumatic fever in 1938. Their passing did not cause a crack in Dietrich's soul, as Vika's did, but it left more of a depressed void that stayed with him, not particularly painful, just empty. Since then, Dietrich was the singular priest here at the cathedral, kept company only by Anna, the church's longtime secretary.

He felt a sense of service as a priest, of course, he still does, yet, there was still that part of him that was waiting to be found out for the fraud he was. He thought, long ago, that confessing to Father Michael all of his shame and secrets would rid him of them. Did he receive forgiveness? Yes. Freedom? Hell no. So he tried to believe the words he said, to try to feel the nearness to God he saw in others. Yet, his past still clinged to him like a shirt after a heavy rain.

Chapter 101
1942 – Present Day, Vienna

The nightmares that haunted him from Munich still kept in close touch with Dietrich; now joined by the gruesome memories of Vika and her children; these were the thoughts and images that kept him falling to his knees before the altar. They had lessened recently, but still came. It seemed all his life, Dietrich would leave places, hoping the things said and done in those places would stay there. They never did. They were forever packing up and travelling with him. Dietrich was meeting with some today, in fact.

"Thank you, Father Praeter, what a powerful sermon today." The young blonde-haired woman clutched his hand and shook it. It was a powerful sermon. He had spoken intensely about God's unwavering love for all men and the spiritual duty as Catholics to follow the teachings of Christ and love all. That God would not abandon us in our quest to do what is right. It seemed to give their withered and worn congregation some much-needed hope; Dietrich so wished he believed it himself.

"Father? Father Praeter?" An elderly gentleman was looking at him quizzically.

"I must have been lost in thought. Please forgive me," Dietrich countered, wondering how long he had been standing there, dazed.

"No forgiveness needed; such a good sermon." He shook his hand and passed on into the street.

Dietrich greeted the last of the congregation of Saint Michael's as they exited after morning Mass. Vienna was so contaminated with persecution and a constant military presence, many people only found solace during that fleeting hour in Mass every day. The crisp air of summer chilled him slightly as he hugged himself against the cold. He gazed out onto the busy street in front of him.

Dietrich thought back to the first of the World Wars, the one Hans and he fought in. He never dreamed there would be another so very soon after.

Although it had been raging for over three years now, the war had just recently come to Austria, and its presence could be seen everywhere. S.S. officers in the streets, transport trucks filled with innocent lives going God only knows where, their only crime being born who they were. All of the crazy ideas spouted in those meetings in Munich now existed as laws. *Where was God in all of this?* That was Dietrich's real struggle with his sermon today. He assured his parishioners, 'God was here,' but he wasn't sure he believed it himself.

A woman caught his eye as she passed in front of the church, dropped her handbag, and smiled as she stopped to pick it up, "Good morning, Father." She picked up her bag and passed on her way. Dear God, did she ever look like Vika.

He still saw her face everywhere, even all these years later, sometimes beautiful and laughing, sometimes just as it was that last time he held her lifeless body in his arms.

Another man, familiar to Dietrich, quickly walked by with a sack full of papers on his back, he stopped his determined pace only to nod an acknowledgement in Dietrich's direction. Dietrich had heard rumors of what was in his pack, and what he did. Vienna had many such leaflets floating around, angering the soldiers, giving hope to the desperate.

Dietrich had been watching him for weeks. He was a completely unassuming man. Neatly trimmed brown hair, always smartly dressed: pressed trousers, shirt, and coat. He had a boyish face; Dietrich would put him around thirty, but he looked younger, innocent. Nevertheless, there had been rumors and he believed them to be 100% true. The idea had come to Dietrich in his sleep and had stayed with him through all his waking hours since the beginning. It was, to him, Divine Intervention. This man was the key. Dietrich knew it. His road to redemption lay with him.

Dietrich walked back into the church. This young man knew him only as his priest, and very generally at that. He always came to Confession on the first Saturday of the month (His confessions gave no hint to secret work; they were always broadly and vaguely stated.) but Dietrich knew if he was to find his own hope, this was the man to help him and the next Saturday was the day it would happen.

Chapter 102

Forgive me, Lord, for manipulating the confessional. However, Dietrich thought he would have God's full approval on this one. He sat behind the screen and waited. His palms were dank and wet as he repeatedly rubbed them against the legs of his black pants. *Fight the fear, Dietrich. Find your peace.*

The young man entered, "Forgive me, Father, for I have sinned. It has been one month since my last confession." It was him, his voice; Dietrich knew he had to act before he lost my nerve.

"No, son, forgive me. I need to talk to you. I know who you are and I know you work with the resistance. I have a way to help." Dietrich paused his rushed words, barely breathing, "I need to help."

He was silent. Dietrich could almost hear his heartbeat racing on the other side of the screen. Nazi spies were everywhere. Could this man trust him? Dietrich waited, knowing the next move had to be his.

"How?" he finally spoke, confident and unapologetic.

"The crypts, underneath the cathedral; I've thought it all out. I am the only one here; I can prepare them without anyone knowing. There is a lot of room. I can help."

More silence followed. He was assessing this priest. Finally, he spoke again, "You realize the danger involved?"

"Yes."

"If you are caught, you may be tortured, yet still, you must not give up any information. You understand this?"

"Yes."

"And know this, no matter what you do or say, make no mistake; if you are caught, they will eventually kill you."

"I know."

Again, he was silent for some time. Then, he asked a very simple question. One that Dietrich wasn't sure he could answer, "Why?"

This time, the silence was his. Dietrich's fear was high, his emotions all over the place. There was his guilt, his anger at those who took his brother from him, his sense of what was right; none of it completely answered this drive that was now inside of him, the one that grew as they spoke to one another. Finally, the only truth Dietrich knew came out, "I need to atone for my sins; I have to get back up."

"Good enough. Get started with your preparations. My name is Josef; I'll be in touch."

Chapter 103

Time moved at the pace of a broken clock. Dietrich waited as patiently as he could to hear from Josef. He had made his decision to take action – finally and was oddly resentful that it was taking so long to begin. He had begun to move small things into the empty tombs below the church: blankets and pillows from the unoccupied clergy sleeping quarters. He swept them clean, and even started a small stockpile of food. The bigger stuff, he needed help with that. And, after waiting so long, Dietrich, frustrated, devised a way to complete it himself. Finally, the first Saturday came and once again, Josef and Dietrich sat in the confessional together.

They met up every night of those next two weeks, after Anna had returned home for the evening and the streets were barren. The repeated trips to the tombs were exhausting and exhilarating. They were able to pry apart the frames on the extra beds, tables, and chairs in the rectory and take them through the tombs in pieces, nailing them back together once inside.

The unused family tombs were such a miracle! Their openings behind their marble family crest were not terribly large, used to push caskets through to the tomb beyond. Yet once inside, there was an enormous amount of space.

Josef thought of things that hadn't even occurred to Dietrich. They sat, finishing the reconstruction of a small bedside table when he spoke, "We need to test the sound down here."

"Why? Who would ever think?"

"Trust me. We need to cover every possible angle. Go back up to the main church. Close me in here. In five minutes, I will scream. I will wait two minutes and do so again. This way, if you hear me, you can come back immediately, so I don't go on. Otherwise, continue around the church, outside and around. Okay?"

"Sure. Great idea. When can we start helping people?"

"As soon as we are certain we are taking them to a safe place. Now go."

Dietrich was far too eager. He knew that. It took him so many years to take a stand and now he wanted so much to do all he could, as fast as he could. Josef helped to keep him focused on the reality of the situation, rather that continually to get lost in the delusion of heroism. Dietrich walked around the church, hearing nothing. He continued outside and sat on the front steps of the church – nothing. As he got up and made his way around the perimeter, an unconscious grin began to take over his face. The silence was the most exciting sound he never heard. This was going to work!

*****

It was so late that sleep was pointless, as the sun would rise in an hour. Dietrich sat, warily on the stone steps leading to the tombs, sharing a rare, but well-earned cigarette with Josef.

"We did it," Dietrich smiled smugly. "I didn't think we could pull it off, but we did it."

Josef looked at him with vitriol, "We've accomplished nothing. Those rooms are empty. People are still in mortal danger out there. And then, when we do get to some, there will still be more, more than we can ever get to." His voice rose as he got closer; Dietrich felt the heat from his breath, "Until this war is over and every one of those sick bastards is defeated, until every person we try and help is safe and free, until then…" He sat back, filled with intensity and defeat, "– we have done nothing."

Dietrich wanted to respond, he did. He wanted to apologize for his grandiose feelings of self-importance, to comfort Josef, but instead, he remained still with shame. Here he was – a priest, and this vagabond was indisputably morally superior to him at this moment. Dietrich had been working toward a selfish goal. He focused on what he would receive from all of this. While this man never stopped thinking of the lives his sacrifice could save. This redemption thing was much more difficult than Dietrich had anticipated.

After a few minutes, the two men got up and made their way upstairs and to the side door of the church. This entrance was hidden from the main street and barred with shrubbery on both sides of the door, in addition to, for the next few minutes at least, the dark of night. "I will bring our first guests tomorrow – seven in all. Leave this door unlocked, as well as the one to the tombs. We will wait for you down there."

Dietrich nodded in reply.

"Father?" The light in the Narthex came on as Anna's voice carried throughout the church, "Father, what in the world are you doing at this time of morning? Who are you talking to?"

Dietrich turned toward Anna, shutting the door in Josef's face to keep him hidden. "Nobody," he smiled, as he efficiently closed the space between them.

"I was just getting some air. You're here early today?" He continued to walk and talk with her, leading her away from the side door and to her office off the Narthex.

"Oh well, Lukas kept me up all night, coughing and wheezing. I didn't get any sleep at all. So, I said to myself, 'Anna, you may as well go to work early and get those quarterly reports finished.'"

"Good thinking, dear girl. I am lucky to be in such dedicated hands." He smiled at her, now standing in her office doorway. She giggled. She was nearing 80, but delighted in his term of endearment.

"Oh, Father, I am far from a young girl." She put her ledgers down on her desk and waved him off.

Chapter 104

It was getting dark outside; it was around nine p.m. Dietrich was going to head over for a late dinner at Beim Czaak and give his sermons some much-needed attention. In the last few weeks, Josef and he had housed fifteen people discretely and safely underneath the cathedral. They were to expect another tonight.

Dietrich sat on the front steps of the church, just watching people, and smoking a cigarette. It was no longer rare, but had become a nightly habit. In times of stress, he fell back to them as some sort of comfort, ever since his time during W.W.I.

Once this war came to Vienna, it never left. The Austrian Republic fooled nobody. They were under German law, and that meant Nazi rule. Seeing Nazi soldiers patrolling the streets in their stiff, pressed black-and-red uniforms, covered trucks coming to take Viennese citizens away, was as common an occurrence as seeing the lad on the corner selling newspapers, or seeing mothers walking their children to school in the mornings.

Some citizens got used to it. Dietrich did. He watched the men, women, and children climb aboard the back of the trucks with their meager suitcases and satchels in their hands. He knew. He knew and they knew that they were not going anywhere pleasant. He saw it the other day in the eyes of a soldier when a woman tripped and bumped into him. He was disgusted, as if soiled somehow by her hand on his chest. He saw it in the hostile movements as they pushed and shoved people into the back of trucks with no room to move, no room to breathe. He saw the same thing in his brother's eyes that last night in Munich: the hate, the disgust, and the absolute desire to punish.

Dietrich watched this hatred slowly grow in his brother: his brother, who fought for their country, his brother, who cried unabashedly for their parents, his brother, who used to pick up every stray animal he found as a child and bring them home to take care of them. His brother became this. Dietrich watched it happen and did nothing (Well, nothing except run away from it as fast as he could). So who really is to blame? Hans for becoming this or himself for letting it happen?

Dietrich looked across the street and saw the empty casings of Jewish-owned businesses (the delicatessen on the corner, Johann's bookstore four storefronts down from there). The front windows of the bookstore were broken and a crude Star of David was painted on the entrance in a mustard yellow, while simply 'JUDE' adorned on the deli. They had once been thriving family-owned businesses, full of hard work, laughter, and love. Now, they were empty, broken, and looted.

*****

An hour later, Dietrich was diving into some delicious Sauerbraten and finally making some headway on this week's sermon, when he heard someone calling his name.

"Dietrich? Dietrich Praeter, is that you?" He looked up to be greeted by a young, petite, fair-haired woman he could not place.

"Yes, I am Father Dietrich Praeter," he responded.

"I cannot believe you are a priest now." She gushed, eyeing his clerical collar, "I never imagined I would run into you here in Vienna." Observing his lack of recognition, she stopped, "Do you remember me? It has been ages."

"I'm sorry, I do not."

"Your parent's bakery in Munich? I always wanted the same thing, even though it took me forever to choose, a chocolate cookie…"

Recognition finally struck him, "Little Eva Braun?"

"Yes!" She clasped her hands together at his successful guess, "It is good to see you. Hans doesn't talk much about you and it is so nice to see you doing well."

"Hans? You know Hans."

"Of course, silly. He works for Herr Hitler. He is a phenomenal officer for the Reich. He is making Germany very proud." She was smiling as she spoke, but it faltered slightly at the end, "Don't you two talk?"

Her change in disposition concerned him a bit, "Well, I just have moved around so much over the years, it had been hard to stay as close as I would have liked."

She seemed to think this over for a moment and then the smile returned, "Well, I have a solution to your problems, then. You see, Hans is meeting the Führer and myself here in a week and we are returning to Germany together. We shall meet with you, right here for dinner, next Friday, say seven?" She paused. This was not a question; almost indiscernibly, there was a change in her demeanor, "I insist." Her smile now lacked its previous light-heartedness.

"Herr Hitler?" Dietrich queried.

"Why yes, Adolf and I are here visiting his homeland for a week. He has business to attend to and I am taking the time to sightsee and take some photos. I do so love the art of photography, don't you?"

Trying to absorb the shock, he kept trying to act appropriately, "Absolutely, a good photographer is worth their weight in gold." This seemed to please her.

"Oh, I do agree. Perhaps I will bring some of my photographs for you to look at next week."

"I would like that. Give my best regards to Hans and… Herr Hitler for me," The word stuck in his throat, pushed by the fear in his stomach, "'til then."

"We will see you next Friday. Until then."

Chapter 105

Dietrich lay in bed, staring at the ceiling for what seemed like hours. His mind raced, he kept trying to gather his thoughts and organize them, to force them to make sense so he could rest. However, they didn't, and he couldn't.

How is it this hard? He was brought up that if you loved and served God, did good things, you were saved. It doesn't seem that hard. It is that hard. The bad things, the people you let down, the evils you ignore, that begins to overshadow all the good you have given. It takes over and plagues you with guilt and remorse. As Dietrich looked back, closer to the end of his life than the beginning now, and realized how many mistakes he had made, how many times he allowed fear to decide his actions, how many opportunities to help that he ignored for the sake of his own comfort. No, of course, it wasn't that blatant at the time. It was justified, reasoned. The missed opportunities to do good, those haunted him the most.

He thought naively; he thought that by joining the resistance, it would all be erased. All the guilt, all the emptiness, but it was still there. He offered the crypts, he painstakingly furnished them, and he went hungry to offer saved food and water. He supposed he thought this would be enough. Change, give, finished. *Not so fast, Priest.* Of all people, Dietrich should know, the giving doesn't end, the sacrifice must continue. One sacrifice is easy; anyone can suffer for a suspended moment in time. Dietrich was a fool. It was the daily sacrifices that trouble. If he was going to make things right, there would be no more 'one-time-only fixes' for his soul. He must dedicate himself completely, utterly to the cause of right, to the cause of God. It was either that or try to live with himself the way things were, and that was not possible anymore.

Here he was, a man of God. People came to him for guidance, he recited platitudes and quoted verses, while the truth was that he just didn't know himself. It took so much more than just trying to be kind and attending Mass every Sunday. There was so much more to it. Doing his best was not enough. Giving of his money was not enough. Leading his flock, the best he could, was not enough.

He didn't save her. He could have. Dietrich could have insisted on leaving the moment she told him her truth. He didn't. He let fear and logic prevail until it was too late. He didn't want a confrontation. He didn't want it to be too difficult. Now, they were all dead. And Hans. *How many ways did I let him down?* Dietrich thought. Too many to count. His failures coupled with the lack of sleep was making him far too self-deprecating. He had to push through. He have not done enough, not for God, not for his fellow man, but now, he could. Now, he would.

Mercifully, his body released itself to sleep. Three-o-clock would come soon and he had guests to meet.

The church was cold and still as Dietrich eventually made his way to the side door. Now that they had refugees there, they kept it locked at all times and met right outside the side entrance. He cracked the door open slightly, looked around, then called quietly, "Josef."

A shadow emerged from the bushes and came toward him slowly, with his head down. It took Dietrich a minute to register that this was not Josef, and that he was wearing a Nazi uniform.

The two men just stood there staring at each other. "Josef sent me. He got caught up and couldn't make it." This man (if he was old enough to qualify for that title) had just heard him call Josef's name a moment ago. This could have been a set-up. This had to be a set-up. It wasn't as if Dietrich had not imagined this type of scenario a million times since embarking on this journey. It just played out so much differently in his mind. He imagined himself stoic, honorable, and steadfast in his convictions. The Nazi officer would be the one with fear in his eyes, for he knew Dietrich would not break.

Not the case here. Nope, here he stood still, wet from the urine running down his pant leg. Not stoic.

"Look at me," the man pleaded. So, Dietrich did, and began to take in the details of the uniform as well as he could in the dark. It was easy to see on closer inspection that this uniform was not the starched, immaculate uniforms Dietrich was used to seeing in the street. This man's was torn, soiled, and stained from what appeared to be bullet holes in the torso. Dietrich looked back up at his face. "Please," the stranger's voice cracked with desperation and then crumpled as he broke into gut-wrenching sobs.

Dietrich knew that people faked their emotions all the time, but this, this seemed genuine. This kind of torment, this inconsolable despair, could not be faked. This, he felt. This man was broken. He was terrified. He was real.

Putting his hand on the man's shoulder, Dietrich led him inside. Holding back from exposing the tombs to him just yet, Dietrich sat him in a pew right in front of the altar. And waited until he calmed down. His sobs finally subsided.

He held out a shaking hand, "I'm Dietrich."

The stranger received it hesitantly, "Jack. Well, Gustav, really. My real name's Gustav, but my mother, she always called me Jack because I was her *Jack-Of-All-Trades*. I seemed to have the talent to know just enough about most things to be very helpful around the flat." He looked wistfully away, "I miss her so much."

"Okay," Dietrich said. "Tell me."

Jack began, "I am what you think I am. That is true, but I never wanted to be." He looked up, keeping his gaze locked on the crucifix above the altar, "The Gestapo came when I was young. They offered small gifts to my mother: fruit, chocolate. They talked about the pride of Germany and of course, about my upcoming roles and responsibility as one of the Hitler Youth. I wanted no part of it. I told them. I was young and stupid and very defiantly told them I wanted no part of it."

"That sounds like the right answer to me."

"Maybe, but I didn't think of my mom. I didn't think of what consequences there would be to my words. We had been able to avoid it for a few years because we were too poor to pay the fees, but then all that changed. I guess, somewhere, I thought they would know I'd make a bad recruit and leave us alone again. I was only fourteen; I thought I knew everything. I didn't know shit."

"What happened next?"

"Nothing right away, the officer told us he was disappointed to hear of my decision and calmly left. A few days later, though, I came home from school and my mother had a black eye and a huge cut on her lip. She also had an eviction notice. She told me 'Jack, don't blame yourself; I'm okay. We will be okay.'"

"What happened to your mother?"

"The same officer knocked on the door that evening to see if I had reconsidered my decision. Against my mother's pleas, I had. Like magic, the eviction notice disappeared and for a few weeks, the gifts came again, until another family needed coercing. They left her alone. At least, that was the case the last time I saw her." His face contorted again, pugnacious with emotion, "I never thought of how my actions would affect her!"

"It's okay."

"Like hell it is!" His contention grew, "That woman never did anything but sacrifice for me. I will never forgive myself if my actions hurt her." He looked at Dietrich and implored, "Please find out what happened to her, how she is? I'll give you all her information, please."

"Okay, yes, I will. But right now, I want to find out how you came to be at my door."

Satiated by Dietrich's compliance to his request, he calmed and continued, "I faked it through the Hitler Youth for four years. I marched, saluted, pretended to buy their bullshit lies. I never thought ahead, you know, of what would happen, after. I found out. I became an official soldier for my country. It had been strongly encouraged. I couldn't fake that so well. I guess, no matter how long you put off taking a side, eventually, the decision is forced upon you. Do you have a cigarette?"

"Come, let's continue this conversation downstairs," Dietrich led him down the stone stairs and sat with him against a wall. He handed Jack a cigarette and a match. Jack inhaled deeply and then continued.

"They assigned me to Mauthausen. Do you know what that is?"

"I've heard things."

"They are all true and that is only the beginning. It's not human! You think you know what happens there, but you don't. You have no idea." His shaking hand sucked deeply on the cigarette, finishing it. Dietrich immediately lit another and handed it to him. He eagerly accepted it and continued, "We arrived with twenty other new recruits and we were sent directly to the officers' quarters. This part was isolated from the actual camp. There were beautifully manicured landscapes; the private's quarters were clean and comfortable. Now, the office we met in, where the Gruppenführer met with the new officers was part of his housing and it was exquisite. Marble flooring throughout, gold embellished chandeliers, it was like nothing I had ever seen. I began to think the rumors of what these camps were all about had been grossly exaggerated. Anyway, we were given our assignments. Two other new officers, Gerald and Leonard, and I were to accompany Commander Mueller and Commander Bauer to the station to meet the new transport of prisoners coming in. It was a smaller transport than usual, and our commandant felt it was an excellent introduction to our duties at the train station. Our commanders stood at attention as we were instructed to each open a cart door and get the prisoners, mostly from Poland and transfers from other camps, into male and female groupings, leaving the children with their mothers. I pulled back the door and was immediately assaulted with falling bodies and the reek of putrid flesh and human waste. I began helping people up that had fallen out, standing them up. For some, there was no help to be had. Commander Mueller came up to help, much more aggressively, pulling out people at a rapid pace and telling them to go to the left or right. He ordered me, 'Take their bags. Tell them they will be given to them later.' I began my next job as efficiently as I could, while my commanders began to separate the men into groups of the young and the elderly. I didn't even think to question why. I found out very soon. We led the group of women, children, and elderly just outside of the restricted camp gates, to a wide-open area, with nothing but a thirty-meter long ditch. It was there Commander Bauer demanded they disrobe. My body was quickly covered in a thick, chilling sweat, and it had nothing to do with the cold temperatures outside. What in the hell was going on? What were we doing? There was no amount of delusion that could keep this reality from my eyes. I was part of this Nazi machine of hatred and death. Bauer walked over to the line, eyeing them, mocking them, and then creating a break in the line. 'You – forward, to the edge of the trench.' The first part of the group moved slowly as they were elderly. There must have been a hundred of them. I stood watching, unable to move. I took in the images before me. These poor people were terrified, they had to be, but they did not show it. They did not hurl back the foul words tossed so casually at them; they did not beg for mercy, they did not cower in fear. They took their last moments to hold and comfort one another, some sang quietly, others prayed. Not one attempted to repay the evil and hate that had been forced upon them. My head vibrated viciously as the gunfire began. Bodies fell into the ditch, toppling one onto the other in their only sign of defeat. Soft tears began to emanate from the waiting groups. Gerald stood near me, equally shaken. Commander Mueller came over to us after the bullets ceased flying. 'These vermin don't deserve your pity. They aren't even human. Now, you are soldiers in the German Army and you will act accordingly.' He sent Gerald to get the next group, which he did. My task was different. 'Here,' he said, handing me his Mauser. 'Weakness is not tolerated. You will lead the next termination.' As I stood there, my eyes fixed on a pregnant woman holding a young girl with one arm and coddling a small boy at her hip. She was singing softly to them in Polish. The boy wrapped himself around her leg as she stroked his tightly curled hair. Her daughter nestled her face into the crook of her mother's neck, allowing her mother to kiss her face sweetly between every verse. This mother, beautiful, strong, and unashamed, found my eyes and locked in, not with hate, but incomprehension. She never stopped whispering her song to her children and she never stopped looking at me. The only time I broke the stare was to take in her burgeoning belly. The baby inside moved and played, pushing little hands and feet to stretch the confines of the womb, contentedly unaware of his or her fate. 'Officer, begin.' Commander Mueller was right beside me. I was to start the gunfire, then the others would join. I raised the Mauser and aimed toward the beginning of the line. This choice, more than any other, would define who I was and where I would be going. I looked back at the young mother, her eyes still locked on me, still singing, still comforting her children until the very end. 'Now!' Barked Mueller, his frustration growing. I dropped the gun. 'What have these people done to deserve this? Look at the children, Commander, so many children!' Seeing nothing but veiled rage in his eyes, I pleaded with the other recruits. 'We can't do this!' I yelled at my fellow soldiers. 'This is wrong! Don't do this! We don't have to do this!' They just stared at me and did nothing. Commander Mueller faced me, calmly picking up the dropped weapon, and striking me across the face with it. 'Get up and join the other undesirables.' I looked around disoriented. I knew there was only one place I wanted to die. I walked down the line a bit and found the woman and her children. 'Aneta,' she said. 'Jack.' Then I took my place in front of them. The first shot burned through my chest as I tried to force myself not to fall back on them. I wanted to remain a barricade for as long as possible. The next one hit my shoulder, tossing me back, against my will, into the ditch. As excruciating pain faded into nothing, I asked God's forgiveness. When I awoke again, it was dark as pitch and silent, except for disembodied cries and moans that died out one by one. Painstakingly, I moved my left arm to retrieve a lighter I remembered was in my pants pocket. I illuminated the area around me and found her, Aneta, still clutching her still children, her belly inactive, with a bullet in her head. I dropped the lighter and passed out again."

Choking back his own emotion at Jack's story, Dietrich pressed him, "How did you escape?"

"The ditch was not guarded. We were hundreds of dead people. What could we do? I waited until dark of night and crawled out. I dug under the fencing and ran. I just ran. Eventually, my paths crossed with Josef. I was hiding under a porch of a pub, hoping to raid their rubbish at dark, when I overheard an exchange between Josef and another man. I understood what they were a part of, and I took a chance."

"Come, I will go get something else for you to wear and let you go clean up." He nodded. Exhausted and starving, Dietrich led him to the water basin around the corner by the sewage drain. He tended to Jack's wounds the best he could which were in surprisingly good condition.

"Exposure to the cold helped them heal. Of course, I still have two bullets somewhere in me. Thank God for small favors, right?" He smiled slightly as he carefully lifted the nightshirt over his head, "Thank you."

Dietrich smiled back, "We have others in hiding. Others who may not take kindly to sharing space with a Nazi officer, regardless of the circumstances. They are frightened. The crypt next to them hasn't been furnished yet, but there are is mattress and blankets and I will bring you some food and water. It may be for the best, until we figure something else out."

"It's more than enough. Thank you, Father."

Chapter 106

Dietrich sat feeling both apprehensive and cathartic about tonight's dinner. He had been thinking and praying a great deal since his encounter with Miss Braun. He needed to go to the rectory and pull himself together before getting ready for his dinner appointment. Beim Czaak was his favorite restaurant in the city, well, maybe not anymore, it inadvertently caused tonight's meeting to happen, and Dietrich was still holding a grudge.

A knock at his door disrupted his thoughts. "Father Praeter, are you in?" He knew the voice before he turned around. This meeting was so desperately more important than the one tonight.

"Yes, Josef, I'm in here," Dietrich responded, as he grabbed the church keys and rose to greet him.

The two men greeted with a hug. A bond such as this was deserving of a bit of emotion.

"The new ones are here with me. I have them waiting in the Narthex. I locked the bolt after we entered." The strong, eager, young lad needed a shave and a good night's sleep. He worked so hard and so nobly with the resistance here in Vienna, and still, he made Mass every day.

"Come, come. Follow me," Jack led Dietrich back the way he came, through the cathedral, and into the Narthex. There, Dietrich saw their new guests.

"Don't be afraid. The Lord is with you and I will serve him justly." There were five of them: a mother and her four children. She had the youngest wrapped in a blanket in her arms. She looked at Dietrich with hesitation. The baby babbled softly and moved about in her arms. She was protectively standing in front of the other children. A boy about twelve years of age peaked around her and assessed Dietrich. Two young girls, one slightly taller than the other, probably five and seven years old respectively, clung to each other without looking up.

The boy finally gathered his nerve and walked around and in front of his mother. "I am the man of our family now. This is my mother, Sarah, and my sisters, Eliana and Ruth." He stuck his badly shaking arm in front of him to shake Dietrich's hand, "Arthur Fisher."

He gave the boy's hand a good strong shake, "It is good to meet you, Arthur Fisher. May I ask where your father is?"

"They took Papa," the smallest of the girls called out from behind her mother, and then dissolved into tears.

"They took him on the last transport, Father." Their mother's voice was alive with grief, "He never would have left willingly."

Dietrich had no response. He simply nodded sympathetically and gathered his new guests, "Follow me to the crypt." Realizing too late how that sounded, he was alerted by the rising of the girls sobbing, "No, no, no, don't be afraid. I have a nice comfortable place for you to stay down there. Come, let me show you."

Even though it was dusk out, they had never attempted to pass the refugees during the day. This was a special case, and time right now was much more important to this family, than protocol was to them. They were still very careful, and confident; Josef assured him that nobody was seen.

Hesitantly, the family followed Dietrich through the sanctuary and down a poorly lit and long flight of stone steps. They entered into the great cavernous area with its exquisite arches and brick walling, it was indeed still a bit macabre. They curved around what seemed like endless corridors, decorated with different crests, near the floor, on the wall. "What are those?" Arthur asked.

"Family crests. They identify the families entombed here," Dietrich answered. Finally, they arrived at their destination. They stood facing the most poorly lit area of the crypt, which would certainly work in their favor. They stood before what looked like just another marble crest on the wall, only it was blank.

"You're putting us in with dead people!" Arthur shouted, terrified, losing all pretense of being the man of the house.

"No, no, Arthur," Dietrich tried to calm him. "This is empty. Well, empty of the dead, there are actually four other families in here. Come, look." Josef came over and helped Dietrich remove the marble plate; it revealed an entrance they could crawl through. Our current guests had arranged the areas into sleeping quarters, a makeshift bathroom and kitchen, and a living area.

Once everyone was in, Josef made introductions while Dietrich checked the food and water supply. An elderly couple sitting in the far-left corner was still shaken from hearing the marble slab move. Their reaction was still one of fear every time they entered. A woman, named Claire (Although he did not remember everyone's names, Claire's had stuck with him), sat on a makeshift bed along the far wall reading *The Happy Prince* to two young chocolate-haired boys in short pants. They were enraptured as she animated her face and changed her voice with each character. She reminded Dietrich of his own mother. That's why she stood out to him, her face, her mannerisms, her heart. Dietrich hadn't thought about his mother much in recent years, but this scene brought back the loss instantly. He stood feeling his wounds until Josef called his name and brought him back.

Dietrich grabbed the waste buckets from the corner and took them back through the crypt opening. There was a sewage and water drain at a room at the end of the hallway that also contained a working sink. He went back in to get the water buckets and made his way down the hall to empty waste and refill water. Dietrich soon returned, handing everything through to Josef and David (one of their guests) before crawling back through.

"Either Josef or I will take care of everything. We will come down and replace water and food as best we can, as well as empty the waste pails. If it is a few days before you see us, do not worry. Our job is to be as cautious as possible to keep you safe. It is better to live with odor or hunger for a few days than be discovered." Dietrich looked around the room. The two young girls were already playing with three other children and some wooden blocks that Josef had found. Two of which were the cutest little four-year-old twins, Gabriel and Gideon Berkman. Eliana accidently knocked over the boys' block tower and they noisily crashed to the floor. Their mother turned to them in panic.

"SHHHHHH!" she reprimanded, terrified.

"It is soundproof down here. There is nothing to worry about. Let the kids laugh and play. It is okay. And remember, this is not forever, the war will end. All wars do. And there will be freedom and light again." Dietrich turned toward Eliana who was clearly still shaken and upset over her accident. He looked her straight in the eyes, "I have something very special for you. Give me a moment and I will go get it." He left and quickly returned to his room and back down to the crypt. Dietrich couldn't afford to be seen or waste time, but this felt like the right moment. He crawled back through and called little Eliana over to him, "I have a very special gift for you. It once belonged to a very special little girl and I am certain she would be happy knowing that another very special girl like you was taking care of it." Dietrich pulled the well-worn rag doll from his cassock, "Her name is Muffin."

Eliana's eyes widened and clutched the ragged doll as if it were a priceless treasure. *If only we could always see things through a child's eyes.* She hugged Dietrich tightly without a word and then ran away to the corner to play with her new friend.

Arthur's mother handed the baby to her son and ran toward Dietrich, enveloping him in a hug, "Thank you. Father. Thank you for saving my children." Now, she began to sob tears of relief. Years of worry over the safety and lives of her children were now given a temporary reprieve.

"What about you?" the older of the two girls, Ruth, asked, "You take care of us, but who protects you?"

Dietrich pointed above his head, "He does. God protects us all. He will not abandon us during this time," saying the words, Dietrich started to believe them a little more.

Ruth persisted. Worry lines taking over her little forehead, her braids slapping her face as she shook her head, "No, that's not what I mean, what happens if the baddies catch you and take you away."

"Oh, I see. Well, Josef and I," he cocked his head over his shoulder at Josef. "We have a system. I have made copies of the church and crypt keys for Josef and four other members of the O5. If something happens to me, Josef will take over. If something happens to him, he has someone else designated to take over. You are in good hands, my dear girl. N, does anyone need anything?"

All heads shook back in response. They had all learned to ration and make do with as little as possible. "Okay, we have to leave. We'll be back soon."

Josef and Dietrich crawled back out, replacing the marble slab. Once back in the Narthex, Dietrich unlocked the main door and confided in his new friend.

"Josef," he recalled the meeting with Eva at the restaurant and shared his dinner plans. "I am worried about how things will go this evening. Please keep your eyes open and take care of those people downstairs if anything happens."

"I will. On my life, I will." He grabbed Dietrich in a hug, "But nothing will happen to you, Father. Now, go clean up, you smell awful!" Josef grinned and Dietrich let out a surprised laugh as his friend left the church. *Time to get ready, ready or not.*

Chapter 107

S.S. men lined either side of the restaurant as Dietrich approached. Hitler must already be waiting. He gave his name and was allowed in. Dietrich stood in the entryway of Beim Czaak, already seeing it differently. This would probably be the last time he ever ate here. He didn't have to look long to spot his table. Hitler did not look much different than he did back when Dietrich first saw him in Munich, in that dirty pub basement. He sat facing the door, while Eva was at his right in a stunning gold-sequined dress. She really was very beautiful. Hans (he assumed it was Hans) sat with his back to Dietrich. His heart jumped. He didn't know if he could do this. Face the powerful world leader he despised – sure. Face the brother he abandoned to him – hell no.

Eva spotted Dietrich, "Father Praeter, come sit." Everyone stood. He knew what was expected next. He hated it, but it was the law. "Heil Hitler," he saluted, as he choked back the bile that rose in his throat.

She waved him over and his feet moved in spite of him. Dietrich sat carefully, greeting Mr. Hitler and Eva, yet hesitant to look at Hans.

"A priest, I would never have guessed that one. Hello, brother," Hans spoke first. Dietrich looked. Hans was muscled and powerful underneath his tailored uniform. He was clean-shaven and had his hair cut short and combed back, his chiseled jaw was set firm. It was clear he had much more to say than he uttered.

"You look great, Hans. It's been too long." With perfect timing, the waiter came to the table to take their orders. Hans ordered Weiner Schnitzel, Eva ordered Goulash, and Herr Hitler ordered Topfenstruedel; Dietrich took Hans' lead and ordered the Weiner Schnitzel, maybe to bond, or because Brim Czaak made the best he had ever tasted.

"So, Eva tells me you are the priest over at St. Michael's in town," Hitler addressed Dietrich; however, all Dietrich could think was that he did not remember telling Eva which parish he oversaw.

"Yes, Führer, I am. I love serving at my parish. I have a wonderful congregation."

"Indeed. It is funny that you mention serving, as a proud German, I can think of nothing greater than serving the Motherland. Can you?" he posed.

"I have always loved Germany. It is my true home," Dietrich responded, wiping his sweating palms on his pant legs.

"Good, good. Maybe you can help me out with a mystery of sorts I am trying to figure out," Hitler responded, as Eva hid a snicker behind her wine glass. Dietrich looked at Hans; he looked at his empty plate.

"I will do my best, sir."

"Excellent, I knew I could count on you." He took a spoonful of sugar and mixed it into his red wine, taking a slow sip; he replaced the glass and looked at Dietrich directly in the eyes, "I took a trip down to St. Michael's Church today and saw no swastikas flying anywhere on or around the church. Many other churches and businesses did this to welcome my arrival and they have continued to keep them up the whole week."

Dietrich listened. He was told of Hitler's arrival before he came, Dietrich knew the protocol as it had been the same since Hitler's visit in '38. He did it before and was even willing to do it again. He did not want attention brought to him or to St. Michael's, but with everything going on, Dietrich simply forgot. This was a major oversight.

He continued, "So can you tell me why your church did not display these flags?"

"Well, it was a complete oversight, Herr Hitler. I will take care of it first thing tomorrow."

"Supporting the Reich is an afterthought to you? Oversights like that can fuel rumors, Father. Those are never good to hear, especially witnessing the fervor that your brother puts into fighting for his beloved homeland." His voice began to rise, "We are doing the very will of God. He is leading my homeland to Germany and smiting our foes." His fist hit the table hard enough to spill wine out of his glass onto the linen tablecloth.

"I mean no disrespect, Herr Hitler," Dietrich looked at Eva, who seemed to be enjoying this as a spectator sport; he looked again at Hans who now was observing the interchange between Hitler and his brother. It was obvious by his facial expression that he did not side with family.

Hitler had calmed himself down, "Good. That is good, I am glad to hear it. Anyone can make a mistake. The important thing is to make it right. I have postponed my departure for another day so that I can see you hang those flags on St. Michael's in all of their splendor."

"You are?" Was this really happening?

"Yes, we will all be by tomorrow morning, before we leave." Hitler turned his attention toward their waiter who was now nearing the table with their food,

"Ah yes, this looks delicious." Hitler changed the subject, and it stayed changed for the rest of the evening.

Dietrich cut his food repeatedly and moved it around his plate, hoping to make it look like he ate more than he really did. Dietrich had a big decision to make, but it wasn't that. It was that he already knew what he had to do, and he hated the consequences that faced him.

Dietrich finally made his excuses to leave, "Thank you for a fine meal, Herr Hitler. Eva, it was lovely to see you again." He turned to Hans as he stood, "I'm so glad I got a chance to see you, brother." Dietrich stuck out his hand.

Hitler was the first to speak, "Hans will be walking you home. It will give you two some time to catch up. I can handle everything from here, Hans." Hans looked as surprised by this announcement as Dietrich was.

He stood and saluted his boss, "Heil Hitler."

Dietrich saluted as well, "Heil Hitler." Hans turned and walked him out the front door.

They walked toward the church in silence for a few minutes. Then, Hans spoke, "How could you disrespect him, the Motherland, like that?"

"What, the flags? I'm going to do it, but it's not right. I don't want to be a part of it," he replied, even with all the years of absence between them, he felt more candid talking with his brother.

Hans looked around quickly, "DO NOT let anyone hear you say that! Put the flags up tonight. He may forgive this."

Dietrich was silent, "I'm sorry I left so abruptly…in Munich. I left what money we had on the table for you. Did you get it?" He brought up the money to justify his cowardly exit. No matter what he did, Dietrich was responsible for his brother. He should have helped Mr. Scheier. He should have stayed with Hans and not left him with no one but that lunatic back in the restaurant. He took a deep breath, "I'm sorry. I should never have left you. I was wrong."

Hans stopped walking. Dietrich realized he had tears in his eyes, "I lost Mom and Dad, and then you. No warning – just gone. I didn't even know where, so I couldn't find you. Why did you do that to me?"

He didn't mention Mr. Scheier at all, "Don't you remember the night I left? What happened?" Hans had no response, "Mr. Scheier died, Hans. You killed him. A harmless old man who fed us and took care of us!" Dietrich was screaming now, not caring ho heard him.

"He was a dirty Jew! He was the reason we were starving in the first place. Selfish, money hungry Kike."

"He was not! He loved you, Hans. He loved you and you beat him to death. He loved me…and I let you. He deserved better than both of us."

"Really, that's what you think?" Hans' sadness at Dietrich's leaving him gave way to anger, "That's what you think?"

"Yes, of course I do."

"Then I'm glad you left, you disloyal son-of-a-bitch." Hans turned and left back the way they had come.

Chapter 108

The Führer himself stopped by, as promised, to see that the Nazi flags hung with pride on the face of St. Michael's Cathedral. Dietrich met him and his regal caravan of cars out front.

"I'm glad to see you have had a change of heart, Father Praeter," he spoke.

"I apologize again for the oversight."

He pursed his lips and tilted his head slightly, contemplating his next words, "That is where we disagree. You see, I don't think it was an oversight at all. Loyalty to one's Motherland is not something so easily forgotten. Do you know what I think, Father Praeter?"

"Please share," Dietrich tried not to betray how dry his mouth had just become.

"I will. I think the rumors are true. Do you know what the rumors are?" he got closer to him, saying this last part in almost a whisper. He was enjoying toying with him.

"Can't say I do, my life revolves around this church; there isn't much room for idle gossip."

Ignoring him, he continued, "The rumors are you are behaving strangely, having late-night visitors, maybe even," he paused and looked around in mock secrecy, "hiding the rats that are trying to destroy us."

Dietrich could barely breathe. He needed to sit down, but anything out of the ordinary right now would be suspect, "I wouldn't do such a thing. I love our Motherland."

He took another step closer to Dietrich, as his S.S. men, including Hans, stepped in closer behind him as well, "Now, I hear you, but the thing is, I don't believe you. I think what is going to happen is this. I am going to proceed with my plans and leave this city with my lovely companion, but I am going to leave some of my best men here to help me sort out this mess." He snapped his fingers and ten S.S. men came to attention behind him, "Commandant Graves, please escort Father Praeter to his office to have a private chat."

"Heil Hitler."

Hitler walked back to his vehicle and turned back to me before leaving, "Goodbye, Father Praeter. I don't see this ending well for you."

*****

"Sit," Commandant Graves shoved Dietrich into his desk chair, "Keys." He tossed his key ring on the desk in front of him. The Commandant was well over six feet tall and built like an ocean liner. He walked around to the front of Dietrich's desk and tried his hardest to be pleasant.

"Help us help you, Father Praeter. Where are the vermin?"

"There is nobody here but me and my lovely Viennese secretary, whom you passed coming in. I am not hiding anyone."

"You are not being helpful, Father. Let's try again." He slammed his palms down on the table in front of him, "Where are the Jews!" He spit in Dietrich's face as he shouted the words. The nice-guy façade was seriously short-lived.

"I can tell you again, but something tells me you won't like my answer."

Commandant Graves stood erect and grabbed Dietrich's key ring off the desk, handing it back to a subordinate S.S. officer. "Search the place!" he bellowed. Looking back at Dietrich, red-faced and furious, he ordered two armed guards to shoot him if he moved and walked out of the office.

Dietrich knew there was no documentation, no correspondence between Josef and himself that would be found. It didn't exist. Unless they suspected the final resting places of the dead, they were in the clear. Dietrich heard them unlocking the door to the tombs and began to pray. What should have been his first recourse was ironically his last.

After hours of desecrating this holy place, Commandant Graves and his men came back to the office, "They may not be here, but we will find them! Make no mistake, they are not safe, and neither are you!"

Dietrich walked behind them as they proceeded out of the church. His legs were so wobbly, he barely made it, but something in him wanted to make sure they left and he locked the doors.

How could they possibly know? We have been so careful. Dietrich's heart broke as he noticed one of the S.S. officers go up to Anna as she left her office and walked into the Narthex. They spoke quietly and she glanced back at Dietrich before they disappeared outside through the large double doors of the Cathedral.

Chapter 109

Dietrich now found himself on his knees in front of the altar. He had always loved the Cathedral. It was here that he felt the closest to God. It was also here that he found Vika: in certain hymns, he heard her voice as unblemished and as lovely as cut glass. Sometimes, in times of the most earnest meditation, he heard her. He saw her; whispering like a school girl in his ear about the life they would share, with her eyes closed to hold onto the dream, biting her lower lip in a childish grin as she described the joy in the children's laughter as they run and play. These memories no longer devastated Dietrich. He knew now, that he would see them again, soon, and then they would have their happily-ever-after. Dietrich hoped he was finally making them proud.

A loud pounding on the church doors jostled Dietrich from his reverie. He already knew who was there. He left the doors unlocked for them; they would enter on their own. He prayed one last prayer, crossed himself, and stood to face his accusers.

What Dietrich did not expect to see was Hans walking determinedly down the aisle. Part of him still denied Hans was really a part of all this, especially here, Dietrich was concerned. By the stern, detached look on his little brother's face, he knew just how wrong he was.

Hans made an impressive silhouette, sharp, and distinguished in his black, tailored uniform. He was followed by four other S.S. officers dressed identically to him. They stopped before Dietrich in front of the gilded altar.

"Hello again, Hans, I've been expecting someone, just not you."

"Dietrich, you did this to yourself when you rejected the Motherland. This is your fault. Nobody can help you now."

"No, I suppose not. However, let's be clear, I love Germany…I love you, Hans. I'm just not willing to go along with killing innocent people to prove it." Hans' fists clenched at his sides and his mouth tightened. He used to do the same thing when he got really angry as a kid—some things never change. For a moment, Dietrich saw his baby brother, angry at dropping his ice cream cone on the ground, as a child in Munich.

"You are so stupid. You just cannot see the truth in front of your face. They are the ones destroying *us*. They are the ones taking from *us*. They are not the victims here! They are the perpetrators!"

"They are people trying to live their lives and raise their children without being persecuted and killed for who they are. And what about me, Hans? What was my horrible crime? Not agreeing with the Führer? I no longer have a choice in my own opinions, is that what great Germany is all about?" Two of the other soldiers came forward toward Dietrich after that, but with a raise of Hans' hand, they stopped in their tracks.

"Father Dietrich Praeter, you are under arrest for conspiring against the Führer and against Germany. Come with us," was all he said, his brother, the one who he helped raise, the one who he went hungry for so they could afford just one class at university, the one Dietrich still loved, despite this.

The chilled air hit Dietrich's sweaty face with welcome relief as they walked out the front doors of St. Michael's. Dietrich made his way down the front steps for the very last time, and patiently stood in line by the waiting transport truck. A small group was already gathered there, bundled in layers, with bags at their feet. Dietrich knew better now, there was nothing he needed to take with him where he was going.

Dietrich looked around at the city one last time. Vienna was so beautiful: the most majestic mountains in the entire world sheathed the city, the crystal waters of the Danube rushed through the middle of town. Yet, most importantly, the nameless, faceless men and women who were still saving the lives of the people hidden in the crypt below our feet were the hidden beauty of this fair city that Dietrich had been lucky enough to see.

Hans gripped his shoulder behind him, just in case Dietrich saw fit to run for it. Dietrich was finally finished running; Hans had nothing to worry about.

"It could have been different," Hans whispered angrily. Whether his anger was still directed solely at Dietrich, or at himself, was unclear.

"I know."

"You didn't have to take it so far."

Dietrich turned to look at his brother, "I am so glad I did." Hans' face took on a look of shock and confusion. He opened his mouth to reply, but was cut off by an alert from another S.S. officer.

"Stop her!"

Dietrich turned swiftly and saw Anna running toward him from around the corner of the church. "Forgive me, Father, please. They were going to hurt Lukas! I was so scared. I didn't know what to do. Please forgive me!" She looked as if she hadn't slept; her face was stained with tears, and Dietrich believed her. He pictured her trauma as the S.S. men threatened her and her beloved, invalid husband. They were the animals, not the Jewish people.

As the soldiers pulled her away from him, Dietrich called after her, "There is nothing to forgive, dear girl."

Soon it was his turn to board the truck. Hans led him down the last of the grand front steps and pushed him forward. *The end had to be soon,* Dietrich thought. This was the fourth transport this week.

He climbed in, careful not to knock down an elderly couple who had just been placed in there before him. Dietrich looked at them as tears came without permission.

The truck began to move and the choices were to hold on or fall. What details Dietrich's future held was unclear, but he knew it wouldn't be good. He knew what the desired end was according to the Nazis. Yet, oddly, he had peace. That quiet, substantiated peace he searched for his entire life, Dietrich found on a transport truck to certain death. He laughed aloud. He couldn't help it. The poor elderly couple took a few steps away from him. Dietrich had no idea if he had found his redemption or not, God would be the judge of that, He always was. But, he knew he found peace, and on his journey, he was able to save a few lives; lives that matter, no matter what the Nazis proclaimed. Now, he saw where God was. He was right here in him and with him. He is the good in everyone trying to help. He is here.

Dietrich stopped laughing (if only for the sake of the elderly couple), but could not break the smile from his face. *Vika, my darling, I see our home and it is magnificent. The children are playing and laughing and you are smiling in the doorway of our small cottage waiting for me.*

I am on my way home.

www.ingramcontent.com/pod-product-compliance
Lightning Source LLC
Chambersburg PA
CBHW072103170626
46813CB00004B/1443